FOR DAD

I Wish You Well

Andrew L. Tierney

authorHOUSE®

AuthorHouse™ UK Ltd.
500 Avebury Boulevard
Central Milton Keynes, MK9 2BE
www.authorhouse.co.uk
Phone: 08001974150

© *2009 Andrew L. Tierney. All rights reserved.*

No part of this book may be reproduced, stored in a retrieval system, or transmitted by any means without the written permission of the author.

First published by AuthorHouse 9/25/2009

ISBN: 978-1-4490-0840-6 (sc)

This book is printed on acid-free paper.

INTRODUCTION

When you wish upon a star
Makes no difference who you are
Anything your heart desires
Will come to you

When you wish upon a star
Your dreams come true.

(Taken from Pinocchio sang by Jimini Cricket)

    We tell our children to always be good little boys and girls and close their eyes at bedtime and wish for something special. Sweet dreams. Children's wishes always come true, don't they.

    But what happens when the adults wish for something.

EXCESS

Chapter 1

The radio alarm bell emit's a loud searing noise, a sound not to dissimilar from a ships fog horn being blasted at full pelt. The noise of course designed to waken the darken room's inhabitants. However as the shrill continues no sign of life emerges from the king size bed which takes centre stage of the small but perfunctory bedroom. The only sign of life is a hand protruding from under the heavy and exorbitant duvet. The deafening ring tones peter out only to be replaced by the morning radios in situ DJ. His tones far from being dulcet in fact altogether far too cheery for 7.30 in the morning. A break for the local news and headlines are swiftly followed by Tears for Fear's illustrative anthem 'shout' The song title not entirely lost on the beds occupant, given the time of day that it is. A slight but none the less noticeable movement from the bed and then the outstretched hand is quickly withdrawn back to the warmth and solace of the all encompassing duvet. The DJ'S voice circumnavigates the room indicating that time has moved on. The time on the clock reads 7.50

The prostrate form in the bed begins to stir again but

this time with a little more purpose. A head appears and with the suns mornings rays already piercing the curtains the persons eyes begin to squint, adjusting to the light so as to focus on the alarm clock. A small groan escapes from it's mouth. Late again.

Mary Kimble slowly begins to sit up. A simple task made all the more difficult by virtue of the previous nights excesses, that being over indulgence with a vindaloo curry and washed down with copious amounts of white and red wine. A thought occurs to Mary, perhaps I shouldn't be mixing the wine and immediately dismisses the idea as a bad one. After all a girl should be aloud some pleasure in life. Except in Mary's case the only pleasure it seems, these days. Mary stares across the bed and ruefully observes her bed has not been shared by anybody else. A disconcerting feeling begins to overwhelm her and immediately she remembers the telephone call she received the previous evening ,the contents of which, brought about her preceding actions and heavy alcohol abuse. The telephone call was from her erstwhile husband and altogether good guy Jeremy, Jez to his friends.

"Hi honey its me sorry for the late call but an urgent meeting has been called and of course I have to attend. The big bosses are coming down and insist the whole team being there and I have been reliably informed that drinks are in the offing so i'll probably stay over in a travel lodge or something similar" Mary was just about to reply along the lines of "oh don't worry about me and by the way give your secretary one as well for me" before Jeremy cut her off simply saving "enjoy your evening see yer" and the line went dead.

Being facetious never was her strong virtue, no she couldn't kid herself any more Jeremy was an all out total pig headed bastard.

Chapter 2

Jez sat in his office feeling extremely tired and fatigued from the previous nights dalliances. It had certainly been an eventful night. He was a natural predator where women were concerned and he used his charm and influence in his workplace to full effect. At 35 years of age Jez prided himself on keeping fit. Daily workouts at the gym and a twice weekly boxercise aerobics class ensured kids, nearly half his age, looked at him with envy. His hair was thick set, jet black and wavy and his face always clean shaven. A thick set jaw line gave him a look akin to a Hollywood actor. At 6ft tall he carried his toned body well and always wore made to measure suits from the best tailors in town. Hardly surprising each of his 30 odd suits he currently possessed cost in the region of £700 a pop. Not exactly cheap potatoes but seeing as his wife had a rich dad, who was he to moan. His eyes were an ocean blue colour and with his dazzling smile and mouth beset with dazzling white teeth he could have graced any catwalk up and down the country.

Born an only son in the heart of London on a rough council estate and to a mother whose only interests were smoking, drinking with her neighbours, Lionel Blair and knowing when her next giro was due, Jez had to fend pretty much for himself. From an early age Jez realised he had a certain attraction to the opposite sex. At the age of 12, Jez had become acquainted with his neighbour's daughter, a girl by the name of Rosie, a not unattractive 16 year old but already making a name for herself on the estate as the ' local bike'. A term Jez was to understand years later. And so it happened on that Sunday morning on his way home from football practice. Rosie had seized her chance and literally grabbed Jez by the stairwell to his flat and without any preamble had set upon herself to take the young boys virginity that morning.

He kind of remembered the fumbling and feeling awkward as he entered her body, but the intense sensation of feeling aroused in a part of his body he only knew to piss with, was certainly at that time a novelty. It had been over and done with in a matter of minutes, in fact he wasn't really sure what had taken place between him and Rosie, she told him afterwards not to say anything to anybody, he promised he wouldn't and that was that. Besides who could he tell. Certainly not his mum, even at that tender age he realised that certain things in life were never to be told to your own mother. It just wasn't the done thing. It wasn't cool. She wouldn't have believed him anyway, she was always remarking to her friends what a dreamer he was and that he wouldn't amount to anything in life. A reference he still today believed of his absent Father, whom he had never known.

A humming noise at the far end of the expansive office brought Jez round from his reverie. Irritatingly he glanced up in the direction of the humming sound and having quickly assessed the time from his Rolex being 7.00am wondered who else would be in the building at this ungodly hour. Jez had always prided himself on punctuality and being the senior accounts manager for

Lindsey and Read, an American financial brokerage firm with offices in London and New York, always liked to be one step ahead from his work colleagues and indeed work rivals .He had in all fairness made it to management level in less than 2 years with the firm and in doing so leapfrogged other candidates whose service with the firm had been a lot longer. It wasn't always one way traffic, working for an American Company had its highs and lows. The work ethic from his employers was always to work hard and be rewarded but also to play hard too. With hard work and a commitment to the cause yes it was possible to go a long way up the corporate ladder however you could just as easily slip back down and he was damned sure he wasn't going to let that happen to him.

The humming noise intensified and Jez decided it was time for a coffee and to investigate further en route to the coffee machine exactly what was shattering the mornings quiet. One thing about Americans he mused, they loved their coffee and the coffee was always on tap and free, ranging pretty much from ordinary coffee to latte cappuccino and mocha with a caramel twist. The list was endless. Jez only took it black, he new that one latte led swiftly to another and before you knew it you were piling on the pounds. His thoughts strayed to his wife and quickly he erased that image from his mind. "Morning Jeremy" with coffee in hand he looked up and noticed an attractive blond wearing a sweat shirt, 2 sizes too large, too hide her ample breasts, he deduced, and a baggy pair of jeans. In one hand she was carrying a mop and in the other a pull along hoover.

"Ah Hi Jeannie its you. I wondered who was making

that infernal racquet" he quipped and flashed her one of his ' I bet you'd love to shag me' smiles knowing she was very happily married. No kids as of yet but i'm sure she and her hubby were having fun all the same.

As Jeannie passed she caught a whiff of his expensive cologne and felt her cheeks begin to redden. Yes he smiled to himself there were indeed other fringe benefits and they came in all shapes and sizes. His particular penchant was fit blonds with big tits.

He sat back at his desk and perused the morning editions. Usual stuff rape of a teenager and man jumping on the tube line. Local have a go hero attempts to stop a burglary at the local Morrissons and was stabbed for his troubles. He let his mind drift back to the previous day when he had met Sandy at the Dog and Duck. He'd finished work earlier than expected and on leaving the building decided to call in to the pub for a quickie. The pub was actually known as the dog and fuck on account of the type of girls who frequented the place. He'd pulled almost every time he visited and last night was certainly no exception. The Pub, not exactly salubrious, but inviting none the less. It reminded Jez of a throwback to yester year, where men would congregate over a pint, tobacco and cigarette smoke adding to the ambience, raucous laughter filling the air, someone guffawing over an old and often repeated joke. Ladies, only on occasions, allowed to enter this mail orientated domain. How the tables had turned, nowadays. The decor hadn't changed an awful lot, but due to the no smoking ban, people hovered outside on the pavement, puffing the cancer sticks as if life were about to imminently end .But nowadays the pub was no longer a haven for men to escape their wives and girlfriends. These days the male hunter had become the hunted. Girls outnumbered the blokes five to one and where Jez was concerned, this suited him just fine. He'd just sat down, pint in his hand and began to survey the talent on show, when almost immediately from his peripheral view he noticed a tall slim blonde and turned to meet her gaze. He smiled his all knowing smile, she looked in her mid forties, her hair bleached once too often, and her make up applied a little too heavily. Wearing a short denim skirt and tight fitted jumper, and leather jacket, she took the seat next to Jez, introduced herself as Sandy and within five more minutes had placed her hand on his thigh. Jez made no attempt to move it, all that was left to do was to phone his wife, make up some bullshit story of an important meeting, he knew she wouldn't object, in fact it was becoming an all together common occurrence, and then let the evenings fun and games begin.

Chapter 3

Whilst still languishing in her bed, Mary thought about her options for the day. Having drifted in and out of sleep she realized that time was soon against her. It was after all 8.30 and to make it to work on time she had to leave by 9.00 at the very latest, as she had to be in the office by 9.30. Over the radio airwaves Wind of Change by the Scorpions began to play. " Behave" she muttered nonchantly, "don't even go there" as her stomach decided to dance an Irish jig, her excessive feast from the previous evening clearly about to play havoc with her digestive system. A pungent aroma escaped and immediately filled the vicinity of the bed and duvet, 'not very lady like' she concurred but what the hell her wayward hubby was nowhere to be seen, so he'd never know anything to the contrary . As her head began to pound, furiously, Mary had made her decision, she was going to throw a sicky and to hell with what her boss thought. Mary worked for a leading Building Society along her local High Street. She'd started off as a junior clerk and never really scaled the heights. She had been with the company for nearly 15 years and she felt she had become one of the furniture almost an inanimate object or was that inadequate. Either way Mary felt she was surplus to requirements. Because of her longevity of service she had rights but more depressingly she believed her bosses felt sorry for her, felt a degree of sympathy. She mainly worked the tills and in doing so had daily and continuous contact with the public. In her mind she was nothing but a 'gofer' a general dogs body. Being called upon to make endless cups of teas for the hierarchy. It pissed her off no end. Having to make banal conversation with Joe public and always having to smile. Well today she didn't much feel like talking to anybody let alone smiling. No they could 'fuck off.' She knew how the system worked in that if she managed to make it into the office and then feigned illness, her bosses would be inclined to send her home, without a blemish on her work record. She knew if push came to shove and she was given the sack, she could turn to her old man.

Her Dad had been a successful property developer and business man. She often joked with him that he had the Midas touch. Everything he touched turned to gold. After 20 years in the property business with investment properties he owned overseas and in the UK he had taken early retirement, to focus his attention now on his golfing handicap and swing. Although handicap being the operative word, he never was that good a golfer, he would often joke that his clubs were indeed his handicap. But it kept him busy and the social life was always a pleasure, never a chore and besides many a deal could still be struck on the fairway and putting green and even the 19th hole.!

He always referred to Mary as his little girl and he would always see her right. Although 'little girl' was stretching it a bit too far these days.

Mary stumbled from her pit and placing her feet precariously on the carpeted floor ambled over to the extension phone, suspended on the opposite wall. Gingerly she picked up the receiver and dialled the office number.

The phone was answered politely and a little too enthusiastically by a young girl called Corrine who was on a work placement from school. Mary asked to speak with her boss Jonathan Mathers, however he was in a meeting with a client and couldn't be disturbed for at least an hour. Mary explained that she was unfit for work, some sort of overnight flu bug, and asked Corrine to pass on her apologies and should Mathers want to phone back could he do so. She hung up.

Chapter 4

Mary approached the en-suite bathroom with trepidation. In fact she always felt the same way when using the bathroom adjoining the bedroom. The en-suite she vehemently believed was the reason Jez wanted the house in the first place. Whilst the bedroom was on the small size, the bed taking up most of the floor space, the en-suite, in contrast was ample and luxuriously appointed. On seeing the house, a brand new one at that, for the first time ,Jez had salivated somewhat on entering the en suite. In fact the agent attending the viewing had commented on as much, alluding to the point that he thought Jez had never seen a bathroom before. Jez had indeed never seen such splendour The only time when on holiday in the States, but not here, not for his own everyday pleasures. The bathrooms he had been used to were always dirty, squalid affairs on account of living in and out of dirty bedsits and having to always, it seemed share a bathroom and toilet facilities with others. The dirt and grime and rank smell emanating from the floors and walls at every turn. To use Jez's paraphrase on entering the bathroom, 'fuck aint this the dog's bollocks' never went down well.

At that time she had glared disgustingly at him and waited for an apology for his outburst knowing it would never materialise. The agent offered an apologetic smile, whilst Jez oblivious to all and sundry proceeded to admire the workmanship of the exorbitant suite with its stand alone shower cubicle with double sliding glass doors, sizeable enough to fit two people in, easily. Matching toilet and pedestal basin with gold inset taps. A separate corner bath with plenty of room to languish in. He ruefully eyed the 'sink unit' on the floor with taps, a quizzical look to the agent and his unasked question, answered, stoically, "that's the bidet, Mr Kimble" and before Jez could reply he continued " I'm sure your wife can explain its function in private" Jez stole a look in Mary's direction and before he could mutter his thoughts 'what a prick' Mary was leading him smartly by the arm and into another bedroom. That had been nearly 5 years ago and to Mary it seemed already a lifetime away. She entered the bathroom knowing what would confront her, once there.

A full length mobile mirror unit stood proudly in the bathroom's corner adjacent to the vanity wash unit, Jez had insisted upon it .She imagined it appealed to his sense of vanity, she could just imagine himself admiring himself in the mirror, in fact she could visualise himself naked in front of the mirror cock in his hand and pleasuring himself. He really was a self centred prick.

Mary stood in front of the mirror and let out a small but audible groan. She had the most amazing eyes, deep hazel in colour in fact just about every body who had known her had commented on such, Jez had told her on their very first date her eyes were dreamy and captivating and that he could swim in her eyes although quite what he meant at the time had been lost on her .On her left cheek sat a small and endearing birthmark.

From a distance it looked liked any other mole found on a body however up close and personal it looked very much like a love heart. In fact Jez in the early days once commented that he thought it had its own heart beat and could see it moving, She wasn't sure if he was pissed at the time but it had felt good though. Now she stared forlornly into the mirror, her eyes no longer vibrant but dull and listless. What stared back at her was no longer an attractive and vibrant person, with a zest for life, but now the mirror reflected back something which was not to his and certainly not to her liking.

Chapter 5

Jez found himself firmly ensconced in a black leather easy chair, situated in one of many alcoves found in the Cafe Noir, a new and trendy coffee restaurant, situated five minutes walk from his office. The morning had passed somewhat unnoticed and now that lunchtime had thrust itself upon him he decided to find some peace and quiet away from the usual cafes and bars littered up and down the road. He had a troubled mind and was feeling perplexed as to why he felt this way. He had a feeling of foreboding, something felt wrong he didn't know what it was but the feeling was there all the same, it wouldn't dissipate. He'd felt like it all morning if truth be told, he'd decided to find somewhere quiet to collect his thoughts. The Cafe Noir was set back from the main drag it was fairly unobtrusive and a comfortable chair could always be found. An eclectic mix of music playing in the background, not loud, but soothing, melodic, giving a person time to think or to hold a decent conversation with somebody, without having to raise voices. In Jez's case time for solitude and sooth a troubled mind. He knew deep down what the problem was: It was Mary.

When he first clapped sight on her he was immediately struck upon how beautiful her eyes were. They were hazel, a colour he had not seen in anybody before, she had almost golden blond hair and was in his eyes pretty fit. That was nearly ten years ago. But now, he couldn't bring himself to say the words on the tip of his tongue, They had litterally jumped into bed the night they had met. It was at a mates wedding and the alcohol as with all these sorts of get togethers had flowed freely. Mary was as it turned out a friend of the bride and Jez a friend of the groom. The wedding was held in a huge country manor on account the brides father had money and wasn't scared of flashing it around. Accommodation was available for those wishing to sleep off impending hangovers and Jez took this opportunity in looking for somebody to share his bed with. It just happened to be Mary. They swapped telephone numbers in the morning and in all probability Jez hadn't really anticipated seeing Mary again. Just another notch in the proverbial bed post. But she had rung! Six weeks later as it turned out. She had a wedding to attend but this time her sister's and she was chief bridesmaid and having not thrown his number away had decided to call him up on the off chance he would like to come. His diary was looking somewhat forlorn that weekend and he'd agreed to tag along. Two weddings in six weeks and the possibility of shagging the same person again left Jez feeling a little like Hugh Grant in Four weddings and a Funeral, he just hoped it wasn't going to be his wedding or funeral in the foreseeable future. The wedding was a gargantuan occasion. No expense had been spared, it transpired that Mary's Father was very wealthy and wanted his daughter to have whatever she wanted. Even if the wedding took place in a castle overlooking the Scottish highlands, again another reference to that film which Jez had duly noted. And so it had come to pass Jez was looking at one of his ambitions in life. The need to have lots of money. Dating Mary from there on in was a given and onto marriage no problem. But that was just it after Jez and Mary were married there indeed was a problem, in fact a fucking huge one.

He stared blankly into his coffee stirring the coffee more times than was necessary. His mind clearly elsewhere. He knew he had a problem where women were concerned, as the song by Robert Palmer famously inferred,you might as well face it your addicted to love, in Jez's case he was stonewall addicted to sex. If it had a pulse and of a consenting age and fit or fairly fit then that was ok by him. But he knew he had another problem. The music suddenly changed and out from the hidden music centre the animals track the house of the rising sun began to play. He began to stir his coffee a little more earnestly 'there is a house in New Orleans' he knew now without a doubt 'its been the ruin of many a poor boy' he felt the feeling wash over him 'and god I know I'm one' Never a truer word he grinned as he left the cafe and made his way back to his office knowing exactly where the afternoon would eventually lead.

Chapter 6

Mary approached the hallway landing with nervous anxiety. She stared down at what had become her nemesis, the stairs. She had to face facts her condition was worsening and if left unchecked who knew where she would end up .With gritted teeth and a steely determination, gripping the handrail she began her descent. Sweating profusely as each foot made its connection with a carpeted step she moved agonizingly downwards. Her movements not at all helped with a raging hangover she was currently nursing. She remembered a time when she could have jumped three steps at a time, up or down and thought nothing of it in the process, but whilst not long ago it might as well been a lifetime ago. Her heart beat increasingly faster each step she took. One slip and she knew she would fall and the injuries she would sustain could be irreversible. She saw in her mind a wheelchair awaiting her arrival and grimly pushed agonisingly onwards, the bottom looming ever nearer. She'd made the descent and felt queasy with the exertions but relieved none the less, that after fifteen minutes and enduring a cardio workout for her troubles she had finally made it.

She was standing in the sparsely furnished open planned lounge come dining room. An expensive three seeter cream leather settee and matching arm chair awaiting her arrival, and not soon enough she thought ruefully, however she had urgent business elsewhere before finally succumbing to the armchairs embrace. She headed off towards the kitchen.

The previous evening her best friend, Andrea and popped round for a quick chat. On her arrival she was carrying a small white box and duly handed it over. Mary instinctively knew the contents of the box and inadvertently found she was licking her lips with anticipation. Andrea's mobile had began to ring immediately she stepped into the hallway, apparently it was her Mum who needed urgent assistance elsewhere, something about her debit card failing at Asda's and with that Andrea had left apologising on the way out and promising to catch up later in the week. The box unopened had made its way into the fridge where luck would have it, it still remained.

Mary entered the kitchen and immediately opened the fridge door. Heaven, she hadn't dreamt it, the box sat proudly on the top shelf of the fridge. She placed her hand around it and extracted it from its seated position and placed the box on the kitchen work top. She slowly began to lift the lid savouring each moment. At last the contents were revealed, inside four assorted fresh cream cakes. What a nice gesture from Andrea, 'I must call and thank her' but that can wait, here was more pressing matters. With her left -hand she pushed the kettle, sitting adjacent the box, on and her right hand began to explore the boxes interior. The kettle began to shrill loudly announcing the water inside had boiled. All that was left of the four cream cakes at this point was a sliver of fresh cream sliding down the corner of Mary's mouth. Her tongue, seemingly with a mind and life force of its own, darted swiftly to its left to hoover up the excess and having retrieved its prize retreated back from whence it had come from. Ah breakfast!! And then Mary Belched.

She decided against making a coffee as the actions to make it seemed too much of an effort, she'd have one later, after her hangover had subsided. She made her way into the living room so she could finally become acquainted with the comfy armchair. The rooms feature mounted on the far side wall was a sony flat screen, in your face television screen. It literally took up the entire length of the wall., what was it she thought? 20 30 40 inches long Christ she had no idea it was just fucking massive. It was of course one of Jez's foibles in life 'the bigger the better' but not where she was concerned of course, that much was plainly obvious. He loved inanimate objects they couldn't answer you back. Especially with his controlling behaviour. He wasn't exactly a bully but then again on second thought he wasn't that far off it either. She wrestled her husband from her mind and proceeded to become enveloped in the embrace of the leather chair. She reached across to the glass top fancy coffee table and picked up one of many remotes parked neatly in a row. The television screamed into life, the noise emitting from its speakers inordinately high. Girls aloud gyrating on the large screen to a new song, the music video channel playing non stop 24 hour music tracks. Mary swiftly turned the volume down to a more respectable level and wondered why her neighbours hadn't complained the previous evening. Then again she decided, they might well have done, she couldn't remember an awful lot from yesterday evening, she was that pissed, it transpired. She grinned to herself, she didn't get along particularly with her neighbours, in fact she despised them immensely, they never said a good morning how are you or anything, a middle aged couple who thought their shit didn't stink, well let me tell you something Mrs!! She dismissed them almost immediately and settled into the chair and began to flick through the channels. The shrill of the telephone woke her with a start and for a moment Mary wondered just where the hell she was, it took a short moment and then she realised. The phone a portable cordless unit sat next to the remotes on the coffee table and she didn't have to stretch too far to pick it up. 'Mary, I got your message this morning'

oh bollocks it was Mathers her Boss checking up on her. She'd forgotten about him altogether. "I'm not over enamoured with your behaviour of late, I want to see you immediately on your return to work"

Not a hello, how are you, just straight to the point as always, she mused. And with that he hung up. He could be a rude arsehole when he wanted to be. 'Maybe I will be for the high jump' a worrying frown beginning to etch across her brow. 'Sod it I'll deal with it later' On the television Fern Britton and adorable Phil Schofield were interviewing Amy Winehouse. She'd just released a new single and the plug was only too obvious. Still, she could bloody well sing, Mary remembered. Jez of course had previously commented about what great legs and tits she had. 'Prick!!!'

Mary turned her attention back to the television . Shit she realised she had fallen asleep and the time was veering nearer to midday. Her overworked stomach began to scream abuse. She focused her attention on Fern and marvelled at how much weight the presenter had lost Ok who bloody well cares she cheated for fuck sake having kept quiet about some operation or other involving a gastric band, Mary wasn't quite sure which, having said all that she looked great bloody marvellous, 'good luck to you girl' Mary offered her opinion to an otherwise empty room, her thoughts again racing all over the place, 'maybe that's the answer, but I couldn't afford it' She thought about her Dad, he'd surely help, but on reflection she knew he wouldn't he was vehemently against what he referred to as 'artificial operations' She remembered a lecture from him at a family party a while back, talking to no one in particular but also to anybody who wished to listen, in, about how people should be proud of who they are no matter what they looked like, god had made them that way and they shouldn't interfere especially as surgery could kill you if not all went according to plan. She loved her dad but he couldn't half be a sanctimonious sod, at times. She let her mind settle there with her dad and with her stomach still screaming for sustenance, promptly fell back to sleep.

Chapter 7

The room was dimly lit, there were no visible doors or windows. The walls, were decorated with tiles, once white and perfect now black and grey with the passing of time. Huge cracks running across its sides giving home to cockroaches and an assortment of bugs and insects never to have been seen by the human eye. The floor cold and unforgiving, human faeces rotting in one of the corners, the blood splattered walls telling its own story of torture and pain. In the centre of the room, bolted to the floor stood an operating table, its edges honed to a razor sharpness, which if touched fleetingly would slice of a finger in seconds. Upon the table a naked body lay motionless, its arms and legs fastened to the table with hard leather straps, tied so tight that seepage of blood was beginning to tear through the epidermis of the skin. Little rivulets of blood already dripping and coagulating on the granite floor. The body was grotesque in its shape, its legs and arms the size of tree trunks with folds of skin overlapping each other forming waves and ripples. Skin from its arms lay loose and flabby, its head a similarity to that of John Merrick otherwise known as the Elephant Man, its face horribly disfigured. It was the body of a woman, the woman stared at the ceiling, with abject horror, her mouth open to scream but muffled by the blood drenched rag stuffed in her mouth, her heart beat filling the cold room.

A figure appeared, from the side, dressed in a doctors gown and wearing a facemask, the figure was carrying a tray covered by a sheet of gauze barely concealing its grim contents. The figure placed the tray at the foot of the operating table and without preamble removed the cloth to expose an assortment of rustic and blunt cutting instruments. The masked figure selected a hacksaw and a butchers saw and held them up to the light so the prone women had a clear view of the utensils on offer. The figure bent down and stared at the woman's arms and with thumb and forefinger of its left hand lifted a flab of skin whilst deftly holding onto the butchers saw. The figure proceeded to slice open the skin with the other saw, its strokes laboured and uneven. Heavy folds of skin fell, from the body, making a slapping sound as it landed on the floor. The woman's eyes appeared to bulge from her sockets, blood began to seep from the corners of her mouth. Her fingers dug into the tables razor sharp edges causing each one to be unceremoniously, sliced off. The masked figure unperturbed took the saw to the woman's face and began to shear away the folds of sweaty skin. The iron taste of the blood now beginning to fill the woman's nostrils, her heartbeat growing faster by the second. As the figure picked up a rusty scalpel and began to delve into the folds of skin that formulated the woman's torso, searching for her life support, her heart, she felt the lightness fade away, the pain beginning to abate as she realised her body was falling into the deep depths of oblivion. Mary woke up.

Chapter 8

Edith Pullman opened the door to the shop. The time was 6.00am. Edith had worked at the convenience store for nearly 30 years and prided herself on never once being late for the morning shift. The shop was a quaint affair, unlike the big superstores with all of the noise and clattering of tills that accommodate these places, no her shop, as she liked to refer to it as, served a small community of people and always with a welcoming smile, even at 6.00 in the morning. The shop called Marchments named after its owner Edward Marchment, who at the grand old age of 85 still kept his hand in, stocked pretty much every item of food and consumables possible. They also ran a small but perfunctory post office, used mainly by the elderly for cashing giros and stamps of course. It was simple just the way Edith liked it. She had to open up the shop at that time in the morning to receive the morning papers. The shop was also a newsagents and confectionary store. Marchments couldn't compete with the big superstores but they had kept their core clients and everybody seemed to be happy with that. Edith was no exception. Edith, with her 65th birthday, looming ever nearer, in fact next month, had always prided herself on looking smart and keeping fit and healthy. However she was the archetypal spinster. In fact she'd written the proverbial book on it. Having never met her Beau in life, had on occasions such as Christmas, found life lonely. She had an upbeat nature, naturally of course, her feelings of woe never lasted that long anyway. She knew deep down exactly why she'd never married.

As a young girl at school from around the age of 14 Edith's breast had grown almost instantaneously overnight. They were huge and became for Edith a great source of embarrassment to her. On reaching adolescence, it soon became apparent to her that boys were beginning to pay her too much unwanted attention. She had dated a few boys, back in the day, but all they seemed interested in of course was her boobs. It drove her to distraction. They all seemed only interested in slipping their sweaty hands up her jumper and having a bloody good grope. She wasn't exactly an intellectual but surely she had something else to offer besides her ample tits. She'd smack them in the face and that always seemed to put paid to their increasing ardour, however on the odd occasion, when she liked someone and thought that perhaps she may be about to embark on a long and lasting relationship, she had acquiesced, however, once her barriers had been breeched, they'd all done a runner in the end. And so it came to pass, Edith decided that men would not play an inaugural part in her life and had settled instead for 2 cats 1 dog and a budgie called Poppet. She observed herself in the mirror languishing on the wall behind the serving counter, and ruefully accepted fate in that gravity had indeed began to take over. What was the saying 'oh yes it all eventually heads south' Indeed this certainly was the case, her 2 biggest friend's had decided quite some time ago, to sag. She sighed. At that moment the door to the shop opened and an elderly gentleman stepped in to the shop's warm embrace.

Edith, on account of her long standing service to the community, knew just about everybody who frequented the shop. Any news about anybody and Edith was 'your girl' In fact she'd become regarded by some as the first port of call for local news, often hearing news first hand from Edith then reaching the news bulletins, on the television, later in the evenings. Yes it had often been said you could always rely on her for news and gossip. She knew everything. Or so it seemed. Edith eyed the elderly gentleman quizzically, he was of average height, still an attractive man for his age, probably had all the girls falling at his feet in his prime, immaculately turned out, it had to be said, he adorned what appeared to be a somewhat expensive if not a little out of place, dark coloured tweed suit with matching waistcoat. Crisp white shirt and bright red bow tie. A little garish Edith bemused. Highly polished crimson brogues finished the ensemble. In his left hand he carried a walking stick, which from Edith's perspective and viewing stance appeared to look like polished ivory. Not that she'd ever seen ivory close up, only on television programmes about elephants and such like, but it was an educated guess and one in which it turned out, she was woefully incorrect about. He wore no noticeable jewellery, and not a tattoo in sight, Edith always thought tattoos were somewhat abhorrent, still most people wore them nowadays, maybe she was a little old fashioned with her views, she knew it was too late too change now. Upon his head he wore an old fashioned, but expensive looking, suede trilby hat. Christ she hadn't seen one of them in years. There was an aura about the man that unnerved her. Yet she had no earthly reason to think like that. The man glanced over in Edith's direction and like something from an old forties or fifties movie dothed his hat in her direction and produced with it the most mesmerising smile she'd ever witnessed. It was captivating. The man walked purposefully over to the counter and greeted her warmly. "Good morning dear lady" and with that he turned around and proceeded to look around the shop. Edith quickly realised he was a stranger, whom she had never clapped eyes on before and with her

curiosity piqued decided she wanted to know who he was and where he hailed from.

" Morning darling" she returned but he had disappeared from her view. Whimsically she decided to set about searching for her prey and to introduce herself to this fine looking gent. It meant leaving the counter and till unattended however she concluded, nobody was likely to come into the shop for a while except the paper man and he never uttered a word, "miserable git".Feeling reasonably safe she set off on her quest. The shop albeit not on the large size encompassed many aisles all the same and when Edith turned around the first of many, the elderly gentleman was nowhere to be seen. It was as if he had literally disappeared. She carried on her search but to no avail. She shouted out "hello" again, the quiet was deafening. She was beginning to wonder if he had snuck out of the shop and her thought's returned to the till and the paper man who was most definitely and now inexcusably late. She turned around, she stifled a scream, the man was standing right behind her. She hadn't heard a sound. His demeanour however, had changed. He appeared agitated and annoyed irritated even.. She couldn't put her finger on it. He just seemed different.

His smile had vanished to be replaced with a deadly looking grimace.

"Are you alright lovey" was all she could think of saying. He didn't reply. Edith's confidence slowly returning, "cat got your tongue love then or what" Still no reply. A feeling of disquiet seeming to overwhelm her. He simply turned around again as if she wasn't even there and began to walk towards the door. This time with anger rising to the surface, she hated rude people, there was just no cause for it these days, marched over and tapped him forcefully on the shoulder

"Listen hear……." he swung his whole body around to face her, he glared at her and the way in which he stared at her immediately stopped her in mid sentence. "I've not come for you" he snarled, his voice seeming to echo around the whole of the shop in fact through to her inner being her soul in fact, and left.

Edith stood transfixed to the spot. Her gaze staring out of the window and staring into nothing. She felt like somebody had invaded her body, she felt sick,. The door burst open and in rushed the paper man with his delivery. He promptly brushed past Edith to reach the counter and deposit his wares. Still not saying or muttering a word or sound. Backwards and forwards with the papers, and a peaceful quiet descended upon the shop as he slammed the door behind him and left. Edith hadn't moved a muscle, in all that time she continued to stare frantically out the window and wondering all the time as to whom or what the visitor had been searching for, with his last words still reverberating around her head and chilling her to the core.

Chapter 9

Mary sat slumped in the armchair. She felt dazed and not a little confused. She had fallen back to sleep. That much she was aware of, but she vaguely remembers the dream. It wasn't so much of a dream but a nightmare of which seemed so vivid it could almost have been real. She knew she was being irrational, 'it was only a dream' flash backs to the dream made her feel nauseous and light headed. The cutting of skin, the blood the feeling of complete isolation and devastation, really felt apparent. But it wasn't, she tried in vain to expunge the images impregnated on her mind, what in hell was happening.? Was it the hangover, surely so, but in all her life thus far, she never dreamt, certainly none she could ever remember. This however seemed omnipotent, as though she was viewing some kind of x rated film but through the recesses of her mind. She looked down at her clothing, she was still wearing her nightgown and cotton fabric dressing gown, from last night and what she saw thoroughly perplexed her. She had been sweating but not like she always had done, when exerting herself. Although she knew just getting out of this chair would prove an erroneous task,. No this was different, profusely so, it appeared, she was soaked through to the skin, it was if somebody had literally poured a bucket of water over her and the buckets had been incessant. She was swimming in it.

She tried to sit up; the leather mixed with her body sweat contriving angrily to pull her back down. The images again replaying in her mind. She closed her eyes as though just by doing so the images would dissipate or at the very least abate somewhat. They had other ideas. The felling of skin, the detachment of fingers and the orchestrater of this macabre scene the masked doctor .The faceless thing going about his gruesome affairs in a business like fashion. She opened her eyes and a piercing scream emanated from her mouth, it felt never ending. Her finger tips gripping the armrests, doing their utmost to impregnate the leather fabric. Exhausted and spent she slumped theatrically back into the confines of the leather chair.

The phone rang. She jumped, her heart seeming to miss a beat. Mary eyed the phone with trepidation, mere suggestion that the person on the other end of the line being somehow involved, too ludicrous to give credence too; but nonetheless the idea seemed a plausible one given the current state of her mind. She needed to calm down, to regain some level of composure. She picked up the receiver, her voice sounding a little too high pitched and nervous. It was Jez.

"Mary you ok? you sound like shit, thought id just check in with you. Before you ask, (she had no intention of doing so anyway) I had a crap night a total waste of time. (She stifled another scream, a vision of a blooded saw invading her mind) I've another meeting to attend I may stay out again i'll let you know, of course, i'd prefer to come home and have a quiet night in, i'm bloody knackered, but you know how these things are…" She didn't but at that precise moment in time she couldn't care less. She couldn't give a shit. She wanted desperately to be somewhere else anywhere for that matter, but it seemed futile the images kept coming back, more detail than the previous; a bloody heart offered by the masked intruder,.... still pulsating.

"Gotta go" The line went dead and this time Mary had no choice, her innards devoid of control, she simultaneously vomited and defecated. Her humiliation complete.

Chapter 10

The elderly visitor left Marchments convenience store with an urgent stride. He felt irritated, it was so unlike him, his attention to detail always faultless. He never made a mistake. It was so out of character. He prided his work on perfection, leaving absolutely no detail to chance, he had made an error. It wasn't altogether particularly problematic, time he knew was on his side, however he was an eternal perfectionist and mistakes were irritating at the best of times. But within the circles he operated he never made an error in judgement. It was unheard of. It was something he knew wouldn't perturb him for long but it was dammed annoying all the same. Even the time opening of the shop, on reflection, he deduced, was far too early for his intended meeting, the likelihood of the person he was acquiring being up at that particular time a guaranteed impossibility. It was still inexcusable, inexplicable even. "I guess these things happen on the odd occasion", he consoled himself. It was certainly a first for him. He reached his car parked in a nearby residential street, just at the time when the heavens appeared to open up and the sudden droplets of rain quickly becoming torrential. He looked up with a mocking grin as if to suggest the futility of natures actions, and found the keys to the hired car in his waistcoat pocket He lingered a little longer looking up to the heavens hardly noticing the wetness of his suit becoming more apparent the longer he stayed out in the open. He realised he hadn't felt this good for an inordinate amount of time and began to relish the forthcoming events yet to unravel, but of which he; unlike the heavens above, had complete and total control over. He settled into the hired car's comfy interior and turned on the engine. He didn't know how long he would use the car for however, he had picked the car up the previous morning and his driving licence and passport documents were to the desk clerk all in order, they were of course all forgeries, he mockingly smiled at the thought of handing over his real identity. That would be interesting he mused and as thoughts of his inconsequential paufax evaporated, the car speed away.

Chapter 11

The cold water rushes through his manicured fingers, he cups his hands forming a bowl like shape to contain the water and proceeds to lift his hands so as to immerse his face in the cool liquid. He repeats this simple but effective action several times and when the task is completed he takes a step back from the plush sink unit and observes ruefully the worried look upon his face .The working afternoon, nearly at its climax, passed fairly noncommittally in terms of problems to solve, in fact had he known to the contrary he possibly could have left earlier on the pretence he had a client to meet, but that was past now. The working day was indeed drawing closer to an end and his goal in sight. Yet he felt an overwhelming feeling of perplexity enveloping him and he couldn't fathom out why. He was by very nature itself a confident person, in fact people who knew him best, often thought he was bordering on arrogant. Its was their look out he couldn't give a damm what people thought if truth be told. He never let anything or anybody stand in his way of success at any level. In those terms alone he knew he possessed a ruthless streak which at times unnerved him. The acquisition of his current car no exception to that rule.He fondly remembered those enjoyable events... His father in law had wanted to buy his wife a car for her 30th birthday and had asked for his assistance in this matter. Knowing his father in law was truly loaded he had persuaded his wife's Dad to buy her a top of the range all singing and dancing Mercedes Coupe 2 seater sports car. He knew the cost price to be in the region of £70,000 and yes it was ostentatious in the extreme but his plan had a ruthless twist in the tale.

And so the birthday girl's party had gone with a swing; family, friends in fact a turn out of more than 300 revellers had been invited and no expense spared. A thought he remembered at the time, a party, that good old Posh and Becks would have given their blessing too. That was the problem with his father in law he never knew when to stop flashing the cash. But he didn't care, he would use her old man for his personal gain. And so onto the grand finale. The car, resplendent with bows and top down, proudly showing off its fabulous interior was presented to his wife by her overexcited supercilious dad.

Her fathers face was an absolute picture of total shame when his daughter, her eyes covered by friends hands, to draw out the surprise and excitement of the occasion, feasted upon this magnificent gift. On opening her eyes floods of tears began to fill her face as she simultaneously fell to the floor in an ungainly heap. Party goers looking on with a sense of both shame and embarrassment. Her Father suddenly realising his massive fuck up. Of course the car wasn't suitable. Why on earth had he not seen it before. His son in law had quickly stepped in to show a sense of unification in the face of utter devastation and with an inordinate amount of smooth talking and a reassurance that the car would be suitable one day for his precious daughter and that he alone should take the responsibility of blame and in effect exonerating his father in law completely from any blame; the keys were duly handed over for him to use as he saw fit.

That was a year or so ago and he still had the car and his wife's dad had bought her a more suitable car and today still grumbling his humble apologies.

The door to the opulent staff restroom, as the yanks like to call it, burst open.

A large and tall man; stood in the doorway obliterating the light from the outside corridor by his massive frame.

"Jez me old mucker how's it hanging"

Jez stood back from the sink unit the taps still running and looked to his side from where the voice had come from.

Michael Dauncey was the office manager. He had total control of some 200 staff and he alone could hire or fire people. If you wanted to get on at Lindsey and Reads this was the man you bowed down to. Even kissed his arse if the fancy took you.

"Having a bash at the weekend to celebrate my new cottage, we just bought. Mind you thought at one time we'd lost it, the owner took a higher bid of £100,000 and we had to better it. I wasn't fussed but the wife had her heart set on it and we don't upset the little ladies do we. What they want they can have. Besides it means I can have a quiet and peaceful life."

Jez grunted an ok but his heart wasn't really in it. He knew what was coming next.

".... and exactly when are we going to see this beautiful wife of yours. Yeah we've seen the picture but come on mate nobody's seen her in the flesh. You know there's even talk about town that your'e not even married. Don't worry, my old son I've quashed those rumours but you know how people are, besides i'd like to meet her myself."

Michael Dauncey had finished his ablutions and started to leave the rest room.

"you know it wouldn't do any harm to further your prospects here mate, the big bosses love family groups." and with his back firmly turned and frame halfway out the door he added, "oh and they love kids!!!"

And with that the door closed leaving Jez alone, the running taps keeping him and his thoughts company.

That was the problem, he surmised, he knew about the party from office chit chat, he wasn't going to let anybody meet his wife, from work, not now, not ever. And as for kids!! The thought chilled him to the bone.

Chapter 12

Mary's face was flushed with the exertions of cleaning up her mess. It had taken an inordinate amount of time and the smell had made her feel even more nauseous. The thought that Jez or anybody, for that matter, might just pop round at that given moment in time filled her with a mortal dread. She was a very trusting person and was always open and honest with people she knew, however, on this occasion her 'dirty' secret would remain just that. She looked down disdainfully at the armchair on which she had been previously comfortable in and now viewed it in an altogether different light. In fact she doubted she would ever sit in it again. A residue of wetness, brought about from intense scrubbing with hot water and disinfectant, was still visible, she knew she had an anxious wait for the chair to 'dry out'. She chastised herself, 'it would have to do' hopefully it would disappear and nobody would be none the wiser, if remnants of her predicament remained she had already decided to throw some hot coffee over it to mask the underlying truth.

She couldn't wait too long. Her exertions had brought upon a ravenous hunger which needed urgently to be satiated.

The night clothes and gown she had been wearing had already been tossed into a black bin liner and waited, now patiently, by the front door to be disposed of far from the confines of her home. She felt sad at the loss of her dressing gown, in particular; it was viewed by the wearer as a 'comfort blanket' in fact not to dissimilar to one of her Dad's pair of white trousers, which as a young child she lovingly remembered, always made an annual appearance for the family summer holiday. Her Dad referred to them as 'his Sydney Green Street's' just who or what were Sydney Green Street's she had absolutely no idea. Dad loved them, her Mum had loathed them and in the end they had had to be thrown out as they were becoming too obscene to wear as the years went by. Bless!

Her ordeal hadn't of course finished. She'd had to clean herself up and that meant taking a trip back upstairs to the bathroom. An altogether different proposition. The bloody stairs again!. Before starting her ascent Mary had a twinge of jealousy towards all elderly people who had chair lifts. 'What a god send' Totally fruitless where she was concerned, of course, she could just see the salesperson turning up at her house armed with briefcase and laptop no doubt, fully expecting to see an elderly or disabled person, a warm welcome expected, to be faced however with,? She let the image go, what was the point she was only deluding herself.

All in all the time she had taken to climb 'Mt Everest' and dress herself had been nearly 2 hours. She hadn't showered, on account to save some time. She'd satisfied herself with a quick wash and rub down, however the sweaty smell of herself still permeated her inner senses and to alieviate the pungent aroma she doused herself, liberally with way too much cheap perfume.

She now stood by the front door her handbag in her

hand and the bin liner in the other. Her lungs protesting at these unfamiliar exertions. In truth she felt she'd run a marathon, not that she'd ever done so, or cared to even consider doing so, but the look on those poor souls crossing the finish line of any marathon event mirrored how she currently felt. Of that she felt certain. Mary knew beyond a shadow of a doubt that if she didn't eat in the foreseeable she would in all probability collapse and die. She stepped out into the outside world.

Her car sat in the driveway, a lavish 4x4 Toyota land cruiser, bought for her by her Dad for her 30th birthday. Albeit after the event. It wasn't that she was ungrateful or anything, but the feeling of hurt and anguish visited upon her every time she opened the car door. She loved the Merc that Jez used but as her Dad always quoted " to never look a gift horse in the mouth" the very thought of actually looking into the mouth of a horse gift wrapped or otherwise, leaving her queasy yet again..

Standing under the outside porch Mary observed dryly the state of the weather. It was far from dry, in fact she had never witnessed weather like it before. The rain was pouring down incessantly and the wind, seemingly of force gale proportions, she surmised, had forced the front door behind her to slam shut. She turned around, more in reaction, offering her hand to prevent the door from doing so, but her movements were too slow. Her overcoat she was wearing would protect her from the elements and fortunately she didn't have to travel too far to the comfort of her car. She pulled open her handbag and inwardly gasped at the realisation she had come outside leaving her car keys hanging on the wall in the hallway. All keys were hung up on the wall, in the inner lobby, a key pad providing the home for car and household keys. It was one of Jez'z ideas he always liked to be neat and tidy.

She felt her anxiety rising to the fore, she searched forlornly into her hand bag, knowing full well the futility of her actions. Her door keys were also hung up on the wall. In her haste to find food she had been, inextricably; locked out.

She could have called a cab but of course her mobile had been left inside. She really wasn't thinking straight, at all. She really was in a predicament. She knew she had no choice in the matter. She needed sustenance and quick. An image began to invade her mind again and she tried to shut it out. Blood and more gore, hanging folds of bloody flesh, swarming with maggots.

Her bile reaching the back of her throat. She swallowed. The act itself making her want to retch again. Wave after wave until she couldn't fight back anymore. Her control again seeming to let her down at every opportunity. She watched with tearful eyes as her vomit washed along the driveway out into the road. Carried along by the relentless downpour of rain. The rain she knew would cover up her waste and for that she felt happy for some small mercies.

But she was now facing a bigger problem than she ever envisaged. She would have to walk to reach her goal, a daunting prospect and one in which she knew she absolutely had no choice with. It was that or wait stranded for her next to useless husband to rescue her. No she could be here all night. She looked ahead at the road and found herself squinting. Visibility was poor due to the deluge and looking up to the sky there seemed no immediate let up, in the proceedings. That was that; she really had no choice. Miserable and with no umbrella, she took a tentative step from the sanctuary of the porch and began to set off on her quest. Immediately wondering what else might befall her already overwhelmingly, disastrous day . She anticipated things couldn't really get any worse for her.

Chapter 13

Jez sat looking out of the car window observing the evenings traffic of people passing by. The car sat almost quietly its engine still on, and yet its melodic rumblings almost impossible to hear. Jez felt supremely anxious, as he always had done on previous occasions, he wanted to leave the car in a safe place, however the environment in which he now found himself was never really safe. It was a part of town that unless you really had to be here you would avoid like the plaque. Kids round these parts ran feral. Even the cops gave the place a wide berth of an evening when darkness began to descend. But that was the problem, Jez had had to come here this evening, he needed to be here, he knew of no other place this good. He had been working himself up all day and his feelings were at fever pitch. When he felt like this he had to see the event through to the bitter sweet end and to hell with the consequences, besides what would be the point of not completing the task ahead, and going home to!!. He quickly expunged the image of his wife from his mind and concentrated back on the street ahead, it didn't bear thinking about. He observed a group of young lads congregating outside the newsagents a little further down the street, no doubt looking to relieve somebody of their wallet as they left the all night store. He looked to his left on the far side to where he was parked and his eyes fell upon the black door with the number 25a clearly emblazoned on it in white paint and not too neat; to put a fine point on it, he mused. As he stared, the door opened and out stepped a middle aged looking man who quickly darted down the street, his head bowed so as not to be recognized by anybody. Jez stifled a laugh, people round here weren't particularly bothered about opening and closing of doors, no the action was on the streets and true too form, as soon as the man was within arms reach the gang set upon the man kicking and punching him as he fell awkwardly to the floor. A swift hand moved deftly to remove the wallet from within his coat and immediately purloined, the gang had dispersed, leaving the man on the floor dazed and confused and nursing no doubt a bruised ego for his troubles in being in this vicinity in the first place. 'I doubt he'll be returning in a hurry', Jez conceded.

The gangs were not too dissimilar to a pride of lions, once fed and satiated, lions were only too happy too leave prey alone until the hunger set them off on the prowl once more. These kids Jez hoped, would escape to an unsavoury location and 'divvy' out their booty. In all probability, he assumed they would use the money for drugs and booze, either way he felt they wouldn't return for a while, gloating over their prize and Jez quietly thanked the man,(who by now had stood up and having dusted himself down had carried on with his journey,) for his kindly but unplanned intervention.

It was now or never and as Jez was unfamiliar with the word never had turned the cars engine off and began to extricate himself from the cars warm enclosure.

The evening had turned cold and with a last and

longing look back towards the Merc Jez pulled up his collar of his overcoat and swiftly made his way to the other side of the street to encounter the black door with its menacing veneer.

One knock and the door was answered and Jez pushed the door unobtrusively to be greeted by its occupant.

Jez entered a small but wide hallway. The decor left nothing to the imagination. Badly stained threadbare carpets greeted the guests on arrival, it may once have been blue but now a mixture of black and grey, torn wallpaper adorned the walls and a musty smell of cheap perfume and sweaty bodies permeated the air. He hadn't come here, after all, to admire the properties interior, he quipped, but the interior of something completely and far more pleasingly different.

"Hello darling haven't seen you in a while" a pleasant voice with a tinge of Polish or Russian dialect dissecting the aroma. The door shut quickly by its enforcer, to deter any further intruders, to the establishment.

"Hi Yana" Jez replied throatily "I've been kinda busy you know" He hated the small talk, besides he had been here not that long ago and she had been the compliant host, but Jez wasn't about to pick fault on the finer details.

Yana, a Polish immigrant in her mid 20's, didn't know and didn't really care, the young man was here and as time was money she knew she would be extracting a wad from him imminently in return for an extraction of only the kind she knew men like Jez enjoyed. She hastily ushered him into a back room. "Please you get unchanged for me soon" Yana struggled with her English yet as far as Jez was concerned was infinitely better than his Polish!! and without preamble she led him to a dirty mattress thrown haphazardly onto the floor.

With much haste Jez threw off his clothing and soon found himself lying face down on the mattress, his face buried in a pillow which by the look and smell of it, had definitely seen better days. But not before he had pressed a wad of ten pound notes into her hand. He cocked his head to one side to observe the young lady.

Jez had frequented this place numerous times before and he knew Yana by name on account of seeing her previously. He imagined this place in all probability had an enormous turn around in young girls plying their illicit trade, either way Jez wasn't perturbed, any old hand would do, providing of course it wasn't his.

Having put her ill gotten gains in a safe place Yana strode seductively over to where Jez lay.

She had long black hair and dark brown eyes. Her face was badly pot marked, as a result of bad acne problems as a child, however the make up plastered heavily on her face seemed only to enhance the poor girls problem. She wore a small denim mini skirt and obligatory black stockings and high heeled shoes. She was naked from the waist upwards. Her pendulous breasts held Jez's attention for a little longer.

Jez turned his head back down into the soiled pillow and let out a muffled sigh as deft fingers began their journey over his legs and back. Kneading and moulding, the fingers and hands going about their business; his senses on fire, he didn't want this to end too soon.

A light tap on his head demanding that it was indeed time to turn himself over. He knew this was wrong, insane even, he was completely vulnerable, he could be attacked, mugged anything could happen, maybe that was part of the thrill of it .Excitement he couldn't obtain elsewhere. His excitement growing by the second as he felt hands and fingers envelope his manhood. Firm strokes and oh so suddenly it was over. Yana already over by the wash hand basin cleaning herself for her next client and Jez left compliant on the bed in a heap, waves of guilt beginning to wash over him. He knew deep down why he came here, and the knowledge held no comfort for him. He quickly dressed.

Yana ushered him out of the front door a little too keenly for his liking, on stepping out onto the street Jez froze in his tracks. He suddenly felt light-headed not from his exertions it was the realisation that his beloved car had been vandalised.

Chapter 14

The elderly man sat patiently and quietly in the comfort of the hired car. He had found a space, and unchallenged had parked the vehicle unceremoniously between the painted white lines.. The parking in this part of town always an issue a growing problem. The streets were littered with permit only bays and the free parking spaces few and far between. The streets were actively patrolled by traffic wardens who were always available it seemed to administer tickets at free will. He had parked in a disabled bay where it appeared a valid disability badge had to be on show. He clearly wasn't disabled but he wasn't going to let that small problem detract him in anyway. A notice board signaled failure to provide a valid badge would result in an immediate fine!.As far as he was concerned he couldn't care less if he received one. After all he certainly wouldn't be paying for it. Let them come after me and the thought brought about a sinister grin upon his face. He stared at the populace as it passed by. People all too busy concentrating on their own lives and nobody else. He knew that in this town young girls had been raped in broad day light and yet in full view nobody had intervened, nobody cared, in fact people were too scared too become involved in other peoples affairs when it was none of their own business. And so it had transpired people were on a daily basis being mugged, beaten up assaulted and worse and in pretty much all cases there were never any witnesses. Oh how he loved this place.

He stared intently ahead and peered at the incessant downpour of rain. He knew it was laughable, futile even, his course was set and nobody could alter that fact His time was coming and his eager anticipation ever growing inside of him. He always felt the same way and let the knowledge of impending intense pleasure course through his body.

He averted his eyes for a moment to the passenger seat and retrieved a small bejewelled trinket box from its seat and held it lovingly in his hands. He looked at his hands, his fingers were long and tapered and manicured. There was not a blemish on any part of his hands his skin taught not loose and lightly tanned, he was pleased with their appearance. He was a perfectionist after all, and his kept immaculate look oh so important.

He opened up the trinket box and viewed its contents. He withdrew a business card and upon it his name in gold leaf lettering. He read the name upon the card and satisfied with what he saw, placed the card in his waistcoat pocket.

He returned his gaze to the outside world just at the time a double Decker bus pulled up opposite and began to unload its burdening cargo.

The time was nearly upon him, his quarry had indeed arrived. Let the fun begin his laughter resonating in the confines of the car.

Chapter 15

Mary stared apprehensively out of the window and reflected on her journey to this point in time which had been tumultuous and nothing short of a monumental task. When she had left the sanctuary of her home she had continuously cursed her stupidness in locking herself out of her house and in doing so had rendered herself immobile, her only available option was to walk, however she loathed with a passion any form of exercise these days and where her hunger was at an all time high she had forced herself into submission that the need for urgent food had won the day over and hence she had embarked on a tempestuous journey, one in which there was no escape or let up from.

She had to make it into town but the journey was some 6 miles away and she knew she would never make that journey unless some form of help was at hand. The only help of course available was the bus service. She didn't really know which would be worse the long and arduous walk or the bus journey. It made no difference if she was being honest with herself. Both options had to be endured if she was going to achieve a modicum of success to her already rapidly declining and onerous day. And so; the rain still pouring from the almighty heavens above she had stoically set off on her cumbersome journey.

The walk to the bus stop was nearly a mile away and

most of it uphill. 200 metres into the marathon and Mary thought her lungs were about to burst with the exertions. Her legs felt like lead balloons each step forced forward more laboured than the previous. Her hair sopping wet and her overcoat failing miserably in its effort to stave off the rain from further displeasure, most notably her black, loose fitting jumper underneath which had infact began to dampen almost immediately she had set off, although damp from the wet of the rain or her own body sweat, Mary was none too sure. Either way she was immensely uncomfortable underneath her coat. There was after all only so much water her coat was designed to repel, she conceded, but not to quell the tornado that she felt was being thrust down upon her. She had upon her feet a pair of soft leather slip on loafers, more accustomed to warmer climes, mainly the interior of the car however today she noticed looking down that a pair of drowned rats would have appeared more succinct a description, in their current predicament. The journey was made far more haphazard due to the relentless wind which lapped continuously at and around her body, her black cotton trousers clinging onto her legs for dear life it seemed.

She had at last reached the bus stop but as the stop itself was not a main stop, but a feeder and request stop only; for the estate on which Mary lived, there was on arrival no shelter to offer respite. She stood up against a brick wall, offering privacy to the garden on the other side, Mary presumed, for some support and tried in vain it would appear to regain back a normal breathing pattern. She knew she would have to endure the long wait for the bus to arrive as the next bus was not due for another twenty minutes and seeing as the buses never ran to time she knew an hours wait was not entirely out of the question. Her wait seemed an interminable one. With still no let up in the weather the wait agonisingly continued. Droplets of rain running down the back of her neck searching for the warm folds of skin, felt like a slow and demeaning never ending torture. But at least; she victoriously accepted, she no longer needed to walk. A car in the distance, caught Mary's attention. It appeared to slow down ,quite considerably and seemed to be heading in Mary's direction. The car edged increasingly nearer, at which point it almost stopped, but at the last second drove past Mary with a real purpose towards an enormous puddle which had formulated by the side of the road. The car driver clearly aware of this had proceeded to steer forcibly the car and purposefully through the puddle. On impact a large wave of dirty water flew from the road and immersed fully the sorrowful figure that Mary cut. The water, black and pungent, drenched her from literally top to bottom and having met its target the car sped off at considerable pace, beeping its horn for the occupants further amusement. Mary began to cry, unashamedly.

As luck would have it; the bus was actually on time and Mary looked to the heavens as if in silent prayer thanking the good lord that her ordeal was nearing an end.

The bus duty arrived and opened its welcoming doors. Mary strained with the effort of stepping onto the raised platform to the interior and as she looked around and took in the view she forced back a groan. There was indeed no where for her to sit down. But then again she had realised that fact long before the bus arrived, she had tried to dismiss the problem to the back of her mind

.She would have to endure the remainder of her journey standing up. Her feet, Mary concluded were about to explode but she had no choice. Having not ridden on a bus for many a year Mary was forced to concede, her troubled day was still not at an end. She paid over her money and with a bemused look upon his face the bus driver closed the doors and navigated the bus out onto the road once more.

Chapter 16

The bus journey had seemed to take an inordinate amount of time. Mary clung to the overhanging hand rail as if her life somehow depended upon it. At one time the bus had veered a little too sharply and in doing so the bus's momentum had knocked Mary off balance and she had stumbled to the floor. She felt a pain tear through her head, the sudden realisation that she had collided with a sharp object on her way down. As she hit the floor Mary cried out, not so much in pain but for the shear embarrassment of the situation she found herself in. She could almost hear her fathers retort 'that's not very lady like' had he been present and witnessed her demise. As she laid on the cold and wet floor Mary realised very quickly that no help would be offered to her. Even the bus driver appeared not to have witnessed the spectacle and had continued his journey as if nothing at all had transpired from within.

Mary had clambered onto her knees and her hands searching for purchase had grabbed hold of a metal pole; joining the floor and ceiling and with a huge, almost Herculean feat had pulled herself to a standing position once more.

Mary continued to stare out of the window, not really taking in the view on offer. Although with this weather on show, there wasn't an awful lot to peer at. Her stomach demanding that it should now take centre stage .The cream cakes she had devoured earlier had provided hardly any sustenance, only a massive sugar rush, but she hadn't really noticed as her hangover had camouflaged any feelings she otherwise had had at that time. Her brain and her stomach were in complete unison demanding she take immediate action. Her stop came into view as the bus took a more sedate turning and as the bus approached, Mary steeled herself, to prevent another fall. The bus came to a halt and its doors opening signalling that it was time to leave. Commuters started to enter the bus before Mary had exited and the bus driver had intervened to let his passenger off. Mary felt light relief at this kindly intervention as she could see with the surge of people entering the bus, becoming all too embroiled by the oncoming tide and not being able to exit.

Thankfully the crowd stepped aside and to Mary's utter amazement a hand had been thrust forward offering Mary an assist in her climb down. Mary had grabbed the beckoning hand forcibly and amazed at her grips strength coupled with the fact the man did not even flinch. She felt she was being thrown a lifeline somehow and the mere fact of refusing the offer would damn her to a hellish eternity. She placed her feet at last on terra firma and observed the man who seemingly had rescued her from falling again. The man was of middle aged, his severely balding head a size too big for his shirt collar. He looked like he worked out on a regular basis, a tan coloured leather jacket trying desperately to hide the bulging muscles underneath but too no avail. He fixed Mary a congenial and yet sympathetic smile and as she offered her thanks the man swiftly leapt onto the bus and quickly disappeared from view. Mary stared back at the bus as it continued its journey, this time fully loaded and realising the rain had began to abate somewhat. No longer were the heavens pouring down upon her, the wind had subsided considerably and looking skywards the sun for the first time today began to make an appearance. Her dampened clothing and sodden appearance momentarily forgotten, her sense of foreboding and ill at ease beginning to slowly lighten, she set off on the last leg of her journey.

Just around the corner and across the road from where she stood, Mary's eyes came to rest upon her holy grail. Her place of worship. Firstly she had to navigate the busy main road, but the recent addition of traffic lights had made this part of the journey a lot less hazardous as it had been on previous occasions. She would often find herself standing on the edge of the road waiting in vain for a lull in the traffic, other pedestrians happy to take their chances by dodging the cars, Mary however, had had to wait always an interminable age to cross, when there appeared to be no cars in the vicinity, yet on all previous outings a car would appear from nowhere and blast their horn unnervingly as Mary would literally freeze rooted on the spot, fearful for her life. It was always the same. People really couldn't care less, especially once behind the wheel of a car. Every languishing pedestrian caught in a cars headlights, like stranded rabbits, were fair game. Mary felt she was the exception to the rule, she was always considerate towards people when behind the wheel of her own car. As the traffic lights signalled red and a high pitched shrill denoting such, Mary had made her way across the road.

Having safely crossed she began to relax, knowing

that immediate relief was just moments away. She stepped firstly into the convenience store to buy herself a paper. She always popped into Marchments for a paper and a chat with Edith, she knew Edith only as a customer to the shop, the woman was always warm and friendly to Mary, one of only a few these days, it appeared, however a young man in his early twenties was currently serving and Edith was no where to be seen.

On asking the whereabouts of Edith, the young man had intimated that Edith had been taken suddenly ill and had left to go home. He wasn't particularly supportive with his comments on the fact and further anecdotes on the matter confirming he thought Edith had done a bunk, pulled a sickie.. Mary thanked him accordingly for his information and armed with her paper left the store, Edith an already distant memory.

Sitting adjacent to the conveniance store sat proudly a building of profound beauty to Mary. The building in question, had been erected on an old car park site, previously owned by the local council, but had been sold off a couple of years back to the highest tender and procured by its now new owners. The building had been erected it seemed in no time and no sooner had the old car park been vanquished good old MacDonalds had opened its doors to embrace the masses. Mary ever since had been one of their most regular customers.

On entering the building a strong smell of quick fried chips and burgers infused with the aroma of coffee permeated her senses and Mary's mouth began to salivate. 'Made it' and she beckoned to the young girl behind the counter for urgent assistance.

Chapter 17

The elderly gentleman observed the melee as passengers pushed and shoved there way onto the bus oblivious to the bus passenger trying in vain it seemed to get off. An intervention of sorts from a kindly waiting passenger and the job of exiting had been completed. He witnessed the woman's struggle to stand alone and viewed her somewhat downtrodden appearance with rousing excitement. Her disquiet and discomfort all too obvious, her inevitable distress only added to his heightening intense pleasure. He waited for the woman to buy her paper, knowing full well the shop assistant had gone home sick. He laughed inwardly, he had that effect on people. The woman left the shop and continued on her journey. He mimicked her laboured and heavy walk across the road with a lightness of foot and alacrity and laughed at his tomfoolery as he followed; at a distance, the woman into the eating establishment.

Chapter18

Mary slumped into one of many soft and inviting chairs available, on account she was the only person currently frequenting the store. The young girl whom had previously taken her order came over to her table, carrying an over burdened tray, with a whimsical look about her face. She placed the tray on the table and immediately dismissed Mary and retired back behind the counter, once more.

Mary viewed the gargantuan feast with beady eyes, her tongue surreptitiously and involuntary caressing her lips. In truth she didn't know where to start. She lifted a handful of newly baked chips, or French fries, using the American colloquialism and without savouring the taste shoved them wholly into her eager mouth and gulped forcibly down her throat. A second and third hand quickly followed dispatched with consummate ease. She retrieved a burger from its box and not withstanding proceeded to devour the burger with zest. Mayonnaise mixed with tomato sauce plopped onto the table as her teeth bit hard into its soft exterior, no sooner had she gulped a sizeable morsel, her mouth already encompassing another large portion. Another plop of mayonnaise and this time her fingers delving into the cool sauce mixture on the table to retrieve the excess.

Eager too continue, her fingers sought out another burger, and the ceremony of eating continued.

Oblivious to her surroundings Mary didn't notice the arrival of an uninvited guest at her table. An elderly gent had sidled into the seat opposite and by his demeanour alone intended to take permanent residence. As Mary continued her all encompassing attack she became mildly aware of a presence occupying her table. Her first thoughts were somewhat bemused and soon quickly becoming annoyance. "The place is sodding empty why have you got too sit here" the words formulated in her mind, however, a huge mouthful; this time a combination of both chips and burger, restricting her vocal cords.

The man sat motionless and stared intently at the woman. His presence began to unnerve Mary. Gulping down another handful of chips she found her voice.

" what's your problem, are you blind or something, go sit somewhere else."

"Its rude too talk with your mouth full young lady" the man returned with an educated accent.

Involuntarily Mary wiped her mouth with the corner of her sleeve and belched as the food hit its intended target. That'll get him moving she deduced, but the man remained impassive. Mary returned to her feast hoping upon hope that if she ignored him he might just up and disappear. Another huge bite and her mouth was back in business again.

"Hello Mary" and her mouth gaped open remnants of partly masticated burger falling into view.

"Ah It would appear I have your full attention now" he quipped and in doing so offered a benevolent and charming smile showing a set of immaculately white and perfectly formed teeth.

"who are you, my long lost granddad or what?" Mary goaded

"who I am is of no importance to you at this moment of time" he profoundly offered,

"but exactly who and what you are is indeed more an appropriate and dare I say a succint question"

"look granddad I don't know who you are but you are really beginning to bug me, why don't you just piss off and go and pester somebody else, can't you see i'm busy and its not as if this place is particularly full, is it"

"oh don't you worry on that account, in good time I shall but right now I would like to become acquainted with you, dear lady and please could you refrain from using foul and abusive language"

A terrifying thought suddenly stopped Mary in her tracks, what if this bloke had been sent by her boss checking up on her, it was just the sort of tricks Mathers had used in the past to find reasons to sack people, have them followed, when he believed somebody had bunked off work once too often; too catch them in the proverbial act so to speak, banged to rights and the rest of course consigned to history

As if he had read her mind the visitor replied

"no I've not been sent by your boss Mr Mathers, although I am acquainted with him, as well"

And before she could reply a look of total bewilderment beginning to etch across her brow, he continued "and no I shalln't be informing him of your current whereabouts or indeed your activities today.... although I must confess" he paused momentarily " whilst your day has caused me much amusement I do not believe Mr Mathers would appreciate the entertainment in quite the same way"

"Exactly how have I entertained you seeing as I've never set eyes on you before" Mary's voice beginning to sound a little angry "what, don't tell me that prick of a useless husband of mine has sent you to spy on me or something like that, no doubt"

"Again you couldn't be further from the truth if you tried,as you might say your'e not even close"

"No Jeremy or is it Jez these days; I understand, has not sent me"

At the shock of hearing her husbands name a spasm caught in Marys throat causing her to cough and remnants of half eaten food flew from her mouth and landed on the seat opposite, missing the man by inches. Most people, Mary assumed, would in all probability have upped and walked out at this stage of the proceedings, however, the man remained impassive, detached from the events unfolding in front of his eyes.

Mary sat, embarrassingly, with her hands in her lap and stared down at her food, on the tray, her appetite beginning to dissipate, somewhat. Waiting like a school child for the berating that a distressed parent would administer.

"lets talk later about your day, but first yes lets look at your food in front of you, what do you see?" Mary didn't answer, her voice had deserted her, she looked glumly downwards not wishing to look at the man anymore.

" shall I inform you" he offered

Mary didn't want to hear it but somehow knew the inevitable would follow.

"now where shall we start, on the table I have counted 3 big mac burgers, 2 cheeseburgers 4 portion of chips 2 large cokes and not too mention the already 2 burgers of which you have demolished" Still Mary sat tightlipped. If she was none the wiser she almost believed this was her Dad in some kind of unrecognisable disguise. But of course it wasn't.

"and of course had it not been for my being here today, disrupting you, no doubt you would have been some way near to finishing by now"

not a peek opposite

" food enough to feed a family let alone just one individual would you not agree"

At this retort Mary snapped out of her reverie and feeling somewhat suitably chastened

"so bloody what, its up too me what I eat and bugger all to do with any body else, let alone you. Just fuck off"

"now, now, there really is no need for language like that is there, I find it supremly offensive, exactly what would your father think?"

"you leave my father out" and Mary retraced her thoughts.

"has my father sent you?" came a nervous reply

"no I am here on my own volition, my own free will and if you wish I can help you"

"help me with what"

"I cannot believe you have to ask that question, look at yourself, are you deluded?.Look in that large ornate mirror hanging on the wall behind me and what do you see?"

Mary's head lifted up ever so slowly and her eyes wandered to the mirror beset on the wall immediately in front of her, she hadn't noticed it before and stared agonizingly at the image portrayed back at her.

" I can't" she muttered almost inaudibly

"so let me"

" if you must"

" correct me please if my synopsis is incorrect. You are looking at a lifeless and soulless individual, one who over the years has become morbidly and staggeringly obese"

Mary looked at the huge fat face, layer upon layer of fat flesh, her folds of skin appearing to form at least three separate chins, her hazel eyes once sparkling with life now dead, resembling dark bottomless pits, her once blond hair full of vitality now lacklustre, dyed a horrible dull brown colour and oily.

The mans words reverberating it seemed all around the shop, amplified in sound, she knew what she saw was real. She wasn't just fat she was grotesque. She burst into floods of tears.

Chapter 19

The double glassed fronted doors flew open and in stepped a group of young students. Their youthful exuberance all too obvious as they approached the counter. Their raucous laughter and foul language filling the immediate vicinity, to the obvious discomfort to the serving girls behind the counter. "Can you please keep the noise down" remarked a pretty dark haired girl, serving, ".....there are other people in the restaurant"

" This aint no fucking restaurant it's a junk food cafe" came a reply from a young man clearly the worse for wear due to the amount of alcohol he had previously consumed and he continued his banter along with his accompanying friends as though the girl didn't exist. His remarks being greeted by a further chorus of laughter.

One young man however, stopped, his attention caught by the odd couple sitting near the front door. He noticed the fat lady was crying and the elderly bloke looked on a little too discourteous for his liking. In fact he looked totally dismissive towards the woman and his uncaring attitude needed addressing, The woman's outpouring of grief was a little upsetting. He approached the table with a steely arrogant swagger.

" oye granddad what's your fucking problem then" as he neared the table his alcoholic breath becoming ever obvious and distasteful. The elderly man shot a sideways glance towards the man and held his stare.. 'Can't you see she's ups.......' the man stopped in mid sentence as his eyes fixed upon the elderly mans stare. The young man stopped in mid track as if he had hit an invisible brick wall. His body froze, his limbs becoming lead weights.

Mary looked up at this unlikely encounter and studied his face and his expression caused her too immediately stop crying. Her mouth fell open and not for the first time today. What she saw on his face was a look of abject terror. Mary peered down towards the floor where he stood, her head becoming queasy, a little nauseous. The man was wearing a pear of tight fitting faded blue jeans and as she stared a dampness began to appear through the denim material, a damp line snaked down his trouser leg and out poured golden liquid onto his white unlaced trainers. A pungent smell permeated the air and the smell of alcohol and urine made for a heady cocktail. Mary thought she had heard the elderly man whisper the word 'leave' but she couldn't be certain, given her confused state of mind. Either way, the effect was instantaneous, the young man blinked as if too affirm his acknowledgement of the instruction and without further preamble turned, swiftly on his heels, and fled the building. Leaving behind him a patch of urine, upon which he had been standing. One of his mates had noticed his demise and quickly followed suit and fled the building. The rest of the group unperturbed by events as non witnesses had completed their orders and left wondering what had become of their 2 absent buddies.

The elderly gent returned his gaze back towards Mary and continued the exchange. 'Now where were we?'

Chapter 20

Jez wasn't a religious person, he had never been brought up believing in a god. He knew other kids he grew up with went to mass on Sundays on a regular basis. No he wasn't at all interested, how could he be anyway. His mum was an out and out alcoholic who didn't give a toss where he was concerned, if he was being truthful, booze and fags were her idea of Sunday mornings and more often than not he would be back from football practice at lunchtime and often his mum would still be languishing in her pit. The smell of cheap tobacco and stale perfume mixed with alcoholic fumes and sometimes puke left very little to the imagination Her bedroom a definite no go area. He could feel himself becoming nauseous just at the thought of it. No back in the day; living with a useless mother, he had had too pretty much fend for himself. Being a particularly observant type Jez often found himself at one of his mates, Dave's mum seemed to spend every waking hour in the kitchen and as his own mum was totally inept in everything associated in this department, Jez found this new area of activity captivating, the smells of raw onions and grilled steaks, freshly baked bread 'mouth-watering' so every opportunity to visit his friends place was keenly accepted and over the years he had become accustomed to every nook and cranny in the kitchen and been taught skills he never knew he possessed. He had for all intense and purposes become a dab hand in the kitchen.

As he stood in the street, now, a cold wind blowing, food was the furthest thought from his mind.Sex always gave him an appetitie but not on this occassion. He viewed his car and cursed. If there indeed exists a god he had certainly dealt out retribution on a massive scale, today as punishment for visiting the prostitute. He knew what he had just done was wrong, but bloody hell, did he deserve this. His thoughts wandered to an overseas trip a few years back.

He had received a telephone call from a friend who had emigrated to the US. Neil had been a friend of his from a young age and had been part of a gang that they had formed, then out of the blue Neil told Jez that his Dad, an engineer and sadly a widower, had been offered a job abroad and the position too good an opportunity to turn down .That was that they said their goodbyes and vowed to keep in touch. And they had.

Neil had invited Jez over for his Dad's 50th birthday party, a surprise, of course and Neil wanted to invite some of his old friends from back home. As it turned out Jez was the only person who Neil had truly kept in touch with and before he knew it he was on a plane, bound for South Carolina. Jez was still a single guy and took off, without a minutes thought.

Neil lived in an area of South Carolina called Hilton Head Island. Not like the Isle of Wight, but an island none the less. The access was a whole lot easier, no ferries to queue up for, a toll bridge and road bridge and there you were. The island was idyllic, warm sunshine all year round, except when tornados, came calling, Neil had informed him .The island apparently didn't just cater for tourists, its long sandy beaches of course, very inviting, and an abundance of golf courses, if golf was your thing, the island had its own residential community, as well. Neil lived with his family in a gated community. To access these areas you had to enter through a security post and unless you lived in the vicinity were not allowed in unless you had a pass.

Neil's home was opulent, something you only saw on television. It boasted 7 bedrooms all with their own private bathroom and a guest room, which had been handed over to Jez to use as he saw fit for his duration of stay. Neil had invested in a time share outfit and had prospered, Neil was never really an extrovert or exhibitionist and had put his success down to his accent. Apparently the yanks just loved the English accent and luck had fallen very kindly on Neil's front door step and had used this trait to full advantage. He was well on his way to becoming a millionaire, fortuitous for his Dad as it happened. His father had been laid off due to an injury sustained at work, Neil hadn't gone into particular detail, however, but immigration would have sent Neil's Dad home if it were not for Neil being able to support his own kind. Neil had married an American girl, Michelle, and she had produced two girls, Becky and Rosanna who at that time were 5 and 7 years old respectively. In doing so Neil was able to obtain his green card and secure his American permanent residency. Much of course to his fathers delight. The guest room, resplendant with its own lounge and kitchen and Jacuzzi bathroom, which Jez had used belonged to Neil's Dad. Jez had often wondered if Neil had married Michelle purely out of necessity, Neil had never alluded to as much but Jez just had one of those feelings that wouldn't dissipate. Michelle had been a congenial host but together there appeared no warmth at all between them. Still fair play, he conceded, looking back he'd had done the same. But he had hadn't he! He dismissed his wife ruefully and returned his thoughts to warmer climes.

The holiday in the states had left a lasting effect on his memory what stood out was the working kudos the Americans enjoyed. They openly encouraged wealth and prosperity. The flashier the car the more an individual was held in high esteem. Expensive Porches and Mercedes cars were all too commonplace. Huge 4x4 Hummers used to cart children off to school in the mornings, all fitted with in built personal stereos and television monitors to add to the comfort. Neil owned all three.

Yes America was big grand and bloody beautiful. Not like here, he returned his thoughts to the present. People were jealous if you had made a name for yourself. He glared again at his beloved car, well possession was after all 9/l0ths of the law and he had no intention in surrendering his car to his wife. But this, was an abomination, he would have to tell the police and his insurance company exactly where he had parked his car and openly omit he had parked in the red light district of town. Mary would find out and accusations would abound. What was he doing there in the first place. The answer only too obvious. She would up and leave him no doubt and he would lose any right to her Father's inheritance. Fuck; it was a bloody mess and so too was the car. The car had been liberally doused with gallons of blue paint and its soft top roof slashed from one corner to another and back again the other side. The paint had been added secondarily and had begun to drip into the cars plush interior and soil the cream coloured leather seats irretrievably. Jez was in a hole and seemingly no way out. This really had turned into one almighty expensive shag and looking up to the heavens as if to ask for help and forgiveness Jez knew it was time to indeed face the music.

Chapter 21

A young girl armed with mop and bucket set about her task to clean the abhorrent mess made on the floor, a look of disgust etched firmly on her face. Mary heard her mumbling something about kids not being able to hold their drink, an expletive followed but Mary had turned her attention back to the strange enigma still facing her. Who are you, the question remained unasked, maybe some things were left unanswered. She eyed the man with real purpose. Mary was no good at guessing peoples ages but she hazarded a guess at the man being mid to late sixties possibly older, but he carried himself as though some 20 years younger. He certainly kept himself fit and she involuntarily stared down at her chubby fingers. The difference oh so stirringly obvious. She returned her gaze and noticed his eyes. They were of deep blue and shone like beacons, they were captivating, in fact Mary studied his face and realised with disquiet that the man looked very similar to her own Dad. He had a kindly face the kind you could turn to when in trouble. His head of hair still thick and wavy, and jet black. Although her own Dad's pate had lost near but all remnants of hair many years ago, but he had too, once upon a time, jet black wavy hair, although nowadays somewhat receding and challenged. If she wasn't mistaken she believed the man obviously had been using a hair dye, natural hair just wasn't that colour. It was too intense. He wore a tweed suit of some description and a dickie bow tie and waistcoat finished off the ensemble. As if reading her mind the man ran his hands evenly through his hair as if to emphasize the point, how well he groomed himself. His face was lightly tanned, either he had been abroad recently or was an addict for sun beds, either way Mary came to the conclusion he was certainly vain.

"who are you?" the words were out at last and sounding a little apprehensive. The man smiled back and leaned across the table, adjusting his posture, Mary noticing his almost brilliant white teeth, his eyes smiling in unison. Maybe he wasn't that bad after all. " If you insist, I know you after all, it is only fair." He reasoned. "You may call me Doctor"

"Doctor who?" her reply was out before she could retract the question sounding a little incredulous at her almost comical remark "Doctor will suffice for now, you need no further information, at present." He returned beginning to sound a little forthright.

"what do you want?"

"The question is not what I want but in fact what do you want?"

"but, before you answer, alas I believe what you want and desire is an impossible dream. Apologies for sounding obtuse but am

I correct in understanding you would like to change your life, in fact your whole body, but with very little effort on your behalf"

Mary didn't reply

"well unfortunately with life's continual changes, a degree of effort and hard work must always be applied. What is it you young people retort" The man looked momentarily upwards searching for the words.

"oh yes I have it now, 'no pain no gain' unfortunately my dear you desire the gain without the pain, with minimal of fuss, so to speak"

" I see by your obvious lack of response I am close to the truth."

"Look Doctor, or whatever you call yourself, I think you should leave" Mary wanted to leave herself if she was being honest, not just to the exit but also to the ladies, and not just to powder her nose. She began to grimace

"My dear girl I cannot yet leave I have only just started"

"started what?"

"your treatment"

"what treatment?"

"treatment to change your life"

Vain and eccentric Mary mused.

"but first you must believe"

"believe what"

"believe in me"

Mary was beginning to lose patience. She really had had a dreadful day and this stranger was really bugging her and she really needed to go to the toilet.

Chapter 22

" look I don't want to appear rude but I think its time you left" Mary said

"so I obviously need to convince you of my credentials" the good Doctor returned. Mary decided she had had just about enough of this interrogation and shifted her bulk in her seat suggesting to the observer she had intentions of leaving imminently. "how was your bus journey today?"

Mary momentarily stopped what she was doing, which wasn't an awful lot, however at this retort she looked at the Doctor and asked a little indignantly "have you been following me?"

" not exactly ,but I have been monitoring your movements, so to speak and very amusing I must admit"

"whats that supposed to mean, not exactly, I'm also glad I offer you entertainment, but quite how I've done that you'll have to explain, seeing as I've never met you before" she responded sarcastically.

" well let me see, where on earth do I start" he sounded a little too jovial

"your bus journey for instance, here today, it appeared somewhat tortuous, you should have sat down, but of course you couldn't could you." " so you have been following me" she interrupted.

He continued ignoring her protestations

" you couldn't sit down, could you? The bus was after all totally empty devoid of any human life all except the driver and yourself, you were the only passenger on board, were you not, but because you are so obese you couldn't occupy any of the seats, the seats are too small for you and when you fell...." he left the statement hanging

"it was undeniably hilarious and very entertaining" Anger beginning to wash over her Mary began to shout "you've no fucking business following me, how dare you"

"I am only imparting knowledge duly observed and there is no need to swear so obtrusively" his remarks seeming to cut her proverbially down to size " shall I continue as I see you wish not to reply further at this point"

Mary shrugged her shoulders it was plainly obvious the Doctor seemed intent on the long haul she decided she just as well play along with the charade. Her need for the toilet momentarily forgotton.

" your soaking by the boy racer, I believe the term may be, whilst you waited for the bus, brought about some merriment, although not to the recipient, I gather"

" big deal, so you have followed me, get to your point" she interrupted again.

"all in due time now please do not interrupt me"

He appeared to be enjoying himself, Mary had decided she on the other hand evidently was not and began to fidget in her seat.

"You locked yourself out of your house, you had no mobile on your person so you really had very little option but to walk, the effort nearly killed you, incidentally when was the last time you took exercise?" The doctor was in full flow now

"and may I suggest to defecate on your chair this morning really wasn't very lady like was it?" The point had just been made, Mary's mouth dropped open yet again, it certainly was becoming a common occurrence today.

" I could of course continue about your day, taking a sick day and as for your breakfast of cream cakes, very delicious" as his tongue teasingly carressed his lips.He was relentless in his fervour "but lets pause for a moment and talk about your husband Jez shall we?"

" Yes lets" the reply came back only just audible and offered through a tight lipped mouth.

Chapter 23

A man and his two children entered the restaurant, his children both girls laughing and holding hands together. Their demeanour suggesting this outing was indeed a special treat and not an everyday occurrence visited upon by others of a similar age. The doctor caught the girls attention and smiled, they returned the same the youngest about 6 years of age, showing the gap in her front teeth and the knowledge to everybody who wished to know the tooth fairy had visited her as she opened her hand to reveal the pound coin found earlier under her pillow.

"do you believe in the tooth fairy Mary?"

The question remained unanswered, almost as if Mary was under some kind of a spell. Today surely wasn't happening, it was only a dream, but as the Doctor's hands enveloped her own and the warmth of his body entering hers she knew this was most definitely and inexplicably for real and not in her imagination.

"I asked you a question, it is rude not to answer"

"what question"

"I repeat myself for the hard of hearing, it would appear, do you believe in the tooth fairy?"

"what sort of question is that"

"a poignant one"

"do you?" he ventured

"of course not its all just bloody make believe stuff for kids isn't it" her voice returning.

"yes of course," the Doctor's reply sounding solemn, "that is your problem, you understand"

"no I don't understand this is all crap a load of bollocks, I thought you were gonna talk about my husband anyway"

"we are, we are, you see neither of you believe or want to believe in children's stories make believe or otherwise,

your husband is completely to blame for your predicament"

" how so is that, I don't understand, you're not making any sense"

"where has your husband been today?"

"at work of course"

"no not just at work in fact as we speak he is about to pleasure himself with another woman"

And before Mary could reply

" he is visiting a prostitute and not for the first time, in fact it has been a fairly frequent occurrence for him" his comments were almost dismissive, as if it were not that important. Mary's head began to pound, this bloke Doctor or whatever he wanted too call himself surely was some sort of looney tune, she reasoned, it was certainly becoming evident he liked to play games.

" look for the last time I want you to leave, my husband wouldn't ....." her voice beginning to sound desperate.

Undeterred the Doctor continued.

"and why might you ask does he entertain himself this way"

" I don't believe you, I don't know who sent you or for what purpose but"

She wasn't allowed to finish her sentence the Doctor had offered up his hand as to silence her and to hear him out.

" children"

" children, children !!!" she repeated agasp " are you saying he's some kind of paedo or what" he let her question float over him and smiled.

" no no, most definitely not, he visits these working girls because he doesn't want children in his life, in short he is incapable of any kind of responsibility he can love them and then leave them in his imitable fashion. He feels safe in the knowledge he will not be fathering any children and therefore has no real accountability to anybody other than himself"

"and I wanted children" her reply strained, tears running down the cheeks of her face

"precisely"

Chapter 24

Jez drove home like a man possessed. It was totally incredulous, beyond belief how anybody in their right mind could destroy 'his car' in such a fashion. He was a man beset with revenge, but not knowing who the culprits were justice would not of course be meted out today. To exacerbate the problem he had been pulled by a patrol car and according to the copper he had been speeding at 50 miles per hour in a 30 mile zone and ensuring for his troubles 3 points on his otherwise unblemished driving licence and a fixed penalty fine of £60 paid immediately, if contested however this of course would no doubtebly be increased by some sanctimonious magistrate wearing a bloody stupid wig and gown. Jez had never been in trouble with the law and had never set foot inside a court house and had no intentions of starting that particular trend now. He resigned himself to paying the fine and accepting the points, but what grated entirely was the fact he was always a very conscientious driver and to his knowledge always kept within the speed limits in around town and on the motorways always staying in the inside lane and overtaking only when it deemed necessary. Had his car not been vandalised he wouldn't have been angry and therefore most certainly wouldn't have been speeding. He rued. The copper had also showed indifference to the plight of his car and suggested he take the car to a garage immediately. Jez promised he would.

He pulled up outside his house and observed the lights were off in fact the house looked completely empty devoid of life. His wife was always home in the evenings, watching some stupid soap or girly programme on telly, apparently she loved these reality big brother shows and as for programmes like the X factor she couldn't get enough of them, she loved how these so called wannabes,(he had heard her use the term before on many occasions) made ridiculous fools of themselves, viewers laughing at their inept performances and cringing at their embarrassments, she loved every minute of it. Jez couldn't see the point. People would stare and point at his wife as she constantly struggled with her own embarrassment towards her weight, the irony not entirely lost on him.

It really was a weird world, and full of nutters he conceded. He noticed a black sack discarded near his front door porch and being of the curious kind volunteered a look inside. The smell hit him immediately, diarrhoea and he had to force down his own vomit as he began to heave. He had a weak constitution where smells were concerned he preferred the smell of expensive women's perfumes, it aroused his senses, he couldn't understand women with babies crowing about changing nappies and getting over excited about the fact. The idea repulsed him. He couldn't think of anything more unsavoury, however looking at the plastic bag he began to think otherwise. A surreptitious glance inside had offered what appeared to be Mary's night clothes and as he placed his door key into the key hole, still holding his breath he began to wonder what other nuggets, for his delectation, would be offered by his overweight and overbearing wife. The door opened. He couldn't wait.

Chapter 25

"Which is why you eat"! The Doctor again lifted his hand towards the now stricken looking Mary, indicating he wished not to be interrupted, "no let me rephrase that, it is the reason you binge eat" Mary was beginning to regain her consciousness of thought, although her head ached like never before and the effort was proving a difficult one. It was as though the Doctor or whoever he claimed to be, was contriving to literally take over her inner thoughts, to control her mind, she shook her head vehemently, she knew she had to get a grip on reality, after all this man had to be a fruit cake, a nutter, yet her subconscious was nagging at her all the time, as this dialogue continued, he seemed to know so much about her, but as for Jez, no way, of that she couldn't bring herself to accept, he surely wouldn't be visiting prostitutes, she'd have known about it surely, but that nagging doubt kept playing over and over in her head, she looked pleadingly at the man opposite her, he returned a pleasant smile, almost as if he could feel her pain her anguish at this torture.

" but Jez" was all she could offer. The Doctors expression changed immediately into a look of total fury. His eyes bore into hers as though searching for her inner being her inner soul, demanding she pay complete and total attention to him.

"I shall not be interrupted again" It was a statement of intent a warning and said with such force and surprised ferocity that Mary felt her hairs on her arm literally stand to attention. For the first time since meeting the Doctor she began to feel frightened in fact a little scared. Her mind wandered back to her earlier thought pertaining to her belief that this bloke was just a harmless old man perhaps looking for company, she began to doubt her first impressions. But what did he want. Mary really wanted him to now leave but she felt her body stiffen on hearing every word almost as if his words alone were somehow nails being driven into her body incarcerating her to the chair, rendering her body immobile. "as I was saying before being so rudely interrupted, you binge eat, do you not?" Mary didn't answer in truth she felt too scared too. "you may answer"

No answer followed, looking still irritated the Doctor clicked his thumb and middle finger of his right hand together, the sound reverberated round her head, it seemed to bring Mary back from wherever she had previously found herself. Had he hypnotised her without her knowledge, the thought played heavily on her mind, was that it he was some kind of hypnotherapist, an ageing Paul Mckenna. It was certainly plausible, but if so what were his motives.

"yes"

was her only reply yet she felt she hadn't answered herself, it was as if the words had come from somewhere else. Perhaps he had drugged her but she hadn't taken a drink since he sat down, she reasoned, this really was turning into a nightmare.

" I see I have your attention again, very good now

listen" again another command and said with some force.

"you eat dare I say like an animal who has never eaten before not out of hunger but to satiate an inner feeling that you have no understanding or control over. It is as if you are trying to fill an empty hole of which depths knows no boundaries has no limits, please correct me if you feel my knowledge is somewhat misplaced, misdirected" His barrage was increasingly incessant. Mary could offer just a small irreverent nod.

The Doctor continued.

"all because you want children and your husband refuses your wishes, what say you my dear" his tone had returned to a more sombre yet pleasant and less threatening one.

" I guess so" Mary had again found her voice almost as if somebody was turning a switch on and off at their leisure, controlling her mind her thoughts her spoken words.

" therein lies the root to your problem, your husband is the catalyst and I can cure it for you, should you desire such an action"

Mary suddenly had a dreadful thought encompass her mind and the words were out before she had control of her senses

" are you suggesting doing away with him, killing him, or something"

" no no you have completely misunderstood me, yes your husband is and has created the problem you now have, had you borne him children and he was indeed susceptible to being a father then perhaps you would not have need of my services, however to address the problem and correct it, you need to change yourself first and in doing so he will conform and change with you"

The Doctor continued and his voice commanding as ever for the recipient to pay yet again full attention to every detail.

" your husband is driven by the need for money, wealth, he yearns it with every pore of his body coupled with the fact he cannot be without female company alas because of your current predicament you have fallen from his so called radar of vision, his feelings sadly are misplaced elsewhere, yet he stays with you because of your fathers wealth and beset with the knowledge that on his death you Mary will inherit an obscene amount of money, enough for you to retire on immediately and your husband will not relinquish that opportunity, he came from a disadvantaged family, of poverty, living from day to day, an alcoholic for a mother a father he never knew, this alone the reason he doesn't want children, he has no idea of showing love or emotion, of being a father and showing responsibility to those who need him most. Giving unconditional love if you please, he simply doesn't know how to, he has never been shown the way. Visiting prostitutes is unemotional for him a complete detachment from reality, a place he can escape to if only for a short time a respite from his inner demons he faces and you Mary can show him the way. But first you and you alone have to change"

The Doctors words had again stunned Mary into a submission of silence and for the first time a pregnant pause ensued, his words hung in the air for an interminable age. The silence was broken as Mary stifled a cry, her voice when it came sounding edgy and raspy, she couldn't believe she was hearing this from a complete stranger.

" how do you know so much and what do you want and why me?"

" simply Mary because I can help and with your permission I shall help, all you have to do is ask me for it"

" I don't believe you my husband wouldn't do those things you have mentioned"

" why don't you ask him"

"oh don't worry on that account I fully intend to"

Mary's blood pressure felt at boiling point. She couldn't listen to this anymore and purposefully lent on the table to gain a vantage point to adjust her enormous bulk.

"I'm leaving now" she interned her bladder fit to burst.

"if you must I am not keeping you" his reply again jovial, comical even and a little mocking.

" you are free and at liberty to leave whenever you wish"

" I have taken the liberty in ordering you a cab which at this present time is sitting outside waiting to take you home, after all" he continued " I couldn't bear the thought of seeing you struggle home this after all the good company you have been today for me, the cab is the least I can offer you. I wish not to appear inhospitable"

Mary found herself at last at a standing position and edging away from the still seated Doctor she replied, forthrightly.

" I don't need your cab I am quite capable of making my own way home thanks all the same" a disconcerting thought again entering her head, she couldn't recall a time when in fact he had called for a cab, she must have missed it.

" don't be so dismissive of me Mary, besides the quicker you can arrive home the sooner you can have a little contra taunt with your husband."

" as I've already told you I will, but let me ask you a question"

" please feel free, be my guest" his hands offered upwards in an expression of acceptance.

" what information do you require?"

" how do you know about Jez's Mum and Dad he has never mentioned his upbringing to me before, every time I have asked him before he dismisses my questions"

" then you need to ask him again but with more authority" Mary was nearly at the exit

" I can't say its been a pleasure but thanks and no thanks"

The Doctor appeared at Mary's side with such speed and alacrity, she couldn't believe her eyes. It was as if time had fast forwarded itself, her eyes viewing events that happened not as of yet, but here he stood, right beside her, his hand resting upon her arm.

"Please Mary I implore you not to be dismissive of me" and with his free hand he offered her what appeared to be a business card of some description.

Unwittingly she took the card from his offered hand, almost as if she had no choice in the matter, her hand having a life force of its own, unanswerable to her now well and truly confused brain.

" you will find a telephone number on the card I have offered, should you wish to change your mind then I will only be too happy too take your call at anytime of the day or night, my time is yours, however if you decide to throw away my calling card then I shall bow down to your acknowledgement that you require no help and bid you a fond farewell"

" Your cab is awaiting" the Doctor held the doors open and pointed to a taxi parked directly in front of them.

" I shall leave you with one last thought"

" and what might that be" Mary asked a little tightly as the Doctor held open the awaiting cabs door its inner sanctum awaiting patiently for the arrival of its new guest.

" how was your nightmare this morning at home whilst you slept on your leather chair"

And with his words resonating in the cabs small but cosy interior, the door closed, its passenger safely ensconced and as it sped away a trickle of urine ran down Mary's leg and onto the carpeted flooring.

Chapter 26

Marys mind was in complete and utter turmoil, not least because of her being visited by the so called Doctor and his unnerving and unsettling words but also for the fact she had involuntarily pissed herself sitting in the cab she now found herself seated.

Her embarrassment heightening as the pungent aroma permeats throughout the cabs interior, it would only be a matter of time before the cabbie stopped and asked her to leave no doubt a dressing down to ensue, yet strangely enough it appeard he was completely impervious from the events unfolding in the back seat of his cab, the car pushed onwards at speed to its final destination.

Mary felt sweat began to seep from almost every pore, her nerve endings heightened to every perceptible sound not just confined to the cabs inner sanctum but it seemed to the whole world parading outside. Cars overtaking at tremendous speeds the noise of their engines accentuated to fever pitch a baby crying in its pram as its Mother waited patiently to cross the busy road, if she was not mistaken she felt she could, unnervingly, hear its little heart beat.

She held a puffy hand to her head to involuntarily wipe a bead of sweat running down her face and into her eye. She felt her brain and mind had somehow extricated themselves from her and were now seemingly enjoying a ride on a fast moving carousel, of which its momentum would never cease. She not only felt nauseous and giddy but sick to the point of throwing up and not for the first time today she remembered.

With an almighty effort of will she tried to concentrate on her uninvited guest and his words spoken to her. But she realised that also was the problem. She had guessed her entanglement with this complete stranger could not have taken place over a great length of time in all probability no more than an hour at worst and yet she could hardly remember a thing about what it was he actually talked about. She felt she was relieving events in a series of mini flashbacks, something about her eating habits and children she couldn't see the connection, her mind racing faster than she could take a breath for pause, what was it about her husband and being a father, something about a bus journey of which she had absolutely no recollection whatsoever of making, God was she going mad, she pressed both hands to her temples as if in a futile effort to massage the pain in her head away. A constant pounding not just in her head but she felt her heart beat racing away, at any moment a heart attack surely must follow.

Another flash, prostitutes, was that it he thought I was a prostitute, he was propositioning me, she concurred but somehow no it didn't feel right, disjointed. She stole a glance to her side, an object had caught her attention and she felt immediate relief at this respite from her inner turmoil. A small card lay discarded on the seat beside her and she placed a hand downwards and lifted it up; between sweaty digits and held it in front of her eyes.

The card looked like any other business card but somehow it felt different. It had a velvet sheen to it, a texture she had never felt on anything before. The card was blank and she turned it over to view the other side. On its reverse side a number jumped out at her. The numbers were in gold and bold the card read 4,18,12,5,22 and 9

As she viewed the card with some bemusement she found herself reading the numbers out aloud and in doing so her headache immediately ceased. Almost as if she had imagined the whole affair. The Doctors words though came flooding back to the fore and she remembered in an instance every word he had spoken. She could at free will replay any sentence back over in her mind when ever the fancy took her. Her husband had been with prostitutes.It had been a clear statememt of fact and not a throw away comment. Her body began to shake and an uncontrollable rage swiftly began to encompass her whole body her whole being.

The car she realised had stopped and its passenger door was being held open by the cabbie. She looked beyond his impassive expression and realised they were parked outside her home.

The man held out a hand to disentangle her from her seated position, on leaving the car two thoughts immediately struck her, she hadn't told the cabbie her address and the smell of urine had completely disappeared, almost as if her accident hadn't happened. But before she could ask the burning question, the car had sped off leaving her with another thought and it wasn't a pleasant one. Her husband. She needed answers and right now.

Gripped by a steely resilience and determination she had never experienced before she made her way headstrong towards the front door. This evening could certainly be enlightening her anticipation heightening as she banged a clenched fist on the front door.

Mary suddenly stiffened, how did the Doctor know about my earlier nightmare. The question ran round her head at breakneck speed, but as quickly as the thought had entered her head it dissipated as the front door swung open.

Chapter 27

As he entered the front room Jez viewed the display on offer with complete and utter dismay and disgust. What in Gods name had his wife been doing. Having a party. Mind you he reasoned, he couldn't blame her even if she had, he could hardly talk, the previous evening he had stayed over at the local premier travel inn and had been literally kept up all night by the voluptuous blonde he had encountered upon earlier at the Dog and Duck, (what was her name again, it had momentarily escaped him) none the less he hadn't envisioned coming home and witnessing what he saw now as an abhorrent disgrace. After all surely his wife could cope without him for one lousy night, ok he challenged, his stop overs had been on the increase recently in fact 2-3 times a week not unheard of, but that in itself didn't give her the right to total the house. His anger hadn't dissipated one jot, with exceptional regard to the plight of his car and seeing the house in its current state just exacerbated his anxiety. The sanctimonious copper with the look of "yeah well whose been a naughty boy then", adding the icing to his cake.

He never felt that he was in some way a kind of control freak or indeed had some form of obsessive compulsive disorder, however he liked things to be in order, put in its place, if things were tidy to begin with then keeping things tidy would prove easier to deal with and surely made sense. An argument to the contrary seemed totally nonsensical. But where his wife was concerned the opposite seemed to apply. Where he was tidy and clean she was the complete opposite. A bloody untidy slob. The large flat screen television on the wall, his pride and joy, was turned on its volume way too loud for an empty audience, the remote controls were strewn haphazardly across the floor, a bottle of wine laid on the floor its contents already embedded into the plush cream carpet, and red wine to boot, the stain laughing back to the voyeur. Discarded cartons containing curry sauce, its food content long gone and digested, adding to the mosaic pattern that had formed with a view for permanent residence. He felt his nausea begin too rise again as a pungent aroma began to permeate his nasal senses. He glanced cautiously around him, searching for the origin of the smell, he stopped dead in his tracks as his eyes fixed upon a stain sitting comfortably on the leather chair. He moved gingerly forward, to further investigate and as he bent down to see a little more clearly his nose beseeching him to bend even further down, his stomach contents heaved as the onslaught of disinfectant diffused with excrement attacked his senses with a vengeance. He barely made it into the downstairs cloakroom, whereupon immediately falling to his knees just about everything he had previously ate and drunk this past week splattered into the toilets bowl. For what seemed like an eternity he remained in a kneeling position. His mind playing over and over again the smells he had previously encountered, not just outside in the plastic waste bag but from the leather chair.. The onslaught incessant. His knees bore painfully into the hard quarry tiled flooring, his hands gripping the toilets edging as if his life somehow depended upon it.

With his head bent down as if in prayer, the torrent eventually ceased and a sense of thanksgiving washed through his seemingly emaciated body.

He gathered his senses and decided upon a journey to other parts of the house. He ventured into the kitchen and a sharp intake of breath took him not by complete surprise if the living room was anything to go by. The fridge door had been left open its contents on offer to any bacteria which happened along. A carton of milk knocked to the floor again its contents spewed along the floor, thankfully along the tiled flooring and a long lasting stain would therefore be prevented, but its residue would doubtless leave behind another smell the kind Jez had had just about enough of today. Another cardboard box lay on the floor keeping company with the milk carton, Jez decided to look elsewhere.

To his chagrin the upstairs faired no better. He viewed the bedroom, he sometimes painfully shared with his wife, the duvet left in a heap on the floor, revealing a large sweat stain on the underlying sheet but what was more disconcerting was the take away box, similar to the one found downstairs, but this had remnants of what appeared to be partially masticated food mixed with its sauce and intact the remainder of its contents upended and liberally it seemed tossed over the sheet covering the bed. Christ, she must have slept in it. The thought repulsed him. An empty wine bottle sat serenely on the bedside table, his anger boiling over, he reached out for the bottle and without purpose of thought grabbed it and drew his arm back, the bottle becoming any inanimate projectile as he was about to hurl it across the bedroom at no particular target. The sound of a car pulling up outside momentarily stopped him in his tracks.

He found himself in no time peering out of the window and a smile began to etch across his face. He suddenly saw another avenue to vent his anger upon and wasting no time at all raced downstairs towards the front door, the wine bottle clutched firmly in his hand with a vice like grip. A heavy thud on the front door denoting that his wife had left her keys behind. Stupid bitch. His free hand reached for the door handle and deftly swung the door open. Unbeknown to him his face a mask of pure hatred and one word on his lips, through gritted teeth. Mary.

Chapter 28

If his face was a picture of abject hatred his wife's face portrayed an either more sinister and angrier one, a look Jez had never in his life seen before, his original momentum coming to an immediate halt as the words from his wife's lips hit him squarely in the face as she stood in the doorway, a clenched fist hitting him squarely in the jaw and knocking him off balance into the bargain simultaneously.

"You fucking cunt, you two time fucking loser, I fucking hate your guts" another blow catching him on the side of his head causing him too flinch. Mary was beside herself with rage all sense of rational had escaped her body .Years of pent up frustration and self loathing becoming a volcanic like eruption. She screamed words from her mouth and making little sense, but the torrent of abuse continued, as if she had no control of her actions whatsoever, as if she was being controlled by an alien entity.

"I hate you, I hate you" repeated over and over until her lungs were fit to burst.

Jez grabbed a handful of hair and forcefully pulled as hard as he could. His mouth tight-lipped, spittle forming on his lips.

" have you gone fucking mad?," as he hurled her body to the floor. Her legs and arms thrashing and kicking in protest, a foot connecting with his upper thigh as she fell, his anger resurfacing.

" The fuck is the matter with you, you stupid bitch" as spit flew from his mouth. His hand still clutching furiously the empty wine bottle, as he lifted the bottle high above his head, his anger overwhelming him. His body tensed as he began involuntarily to bring the bottle down upon its unwitting victim laying on the floor.

"NOOOOOOOOOO" Mary's hand raised instinctively in front of her face for protection from a beating she knew she couldn't avoid. She closed her eyes and waited for the bottle to crack upon her upturned face. It never came.

Mary's words seemed to reach somewhere inside of Jez's head, searching out for the good in him, he had never in his life hit a woman and somehow as a final retrieve her words prevented him from committing this heinous crime for the first time.

Jez literally froze to the spot as the words found their intended target, the realisation of what he was about to commit becoming increasingly evident, he relaxed his grip on the bottle but not entirely so, bringing the bottle down to his side.

He stared open mouthed at the prostrate form of his wife on the floor and as the proverbial red mist began to clear his anger being quickly replaced by guilt and remorse, he stepped over the body and walked slowly into the living room and without preamble fell heavily into the leather settee, the bottle he placed carefully onto the glass top coffee table as if the bottle was some kind of fragile ornament its value priceless.

He ran his hands through his hair and as he brought

them back to his face to mask his guilt he began to sob into them, his head bowed down in an act of total revulsion and humiliation at his previous actions. Mary witnessed the sight of her husband begin to cry; a sight she had never seen before, as she too stepped into the living room, and not for the first time today, she recalled her mouth fell open at this moving act of humility.

She reached a hand out to steady herself and too fell into the leather chair sitting directly opposite where her husband sat slumped, little realising she had just broken a promise a vow never to sit in this particular seat again, the same seat she had humiliated herself in earlier in the day.

Mary looked almost apologetically at her husband as if her actions had been precipitated by him alone.

"Why?"

The question hung in the air for an interminable age.

"Why?" She found herself repeating the question her voice sounding edgy and nervous not really wanting him to answer if truth be told.

Jez looked sorrowfully at his wife a look of bewilderment and confusion etched into his handsome features.

"why what" was all he could reply. He was in truth completely at a loss as to the last 5 minutes of his life and to how the events had become to play out this particular scene.

She found herself staring at her husband the words refusing to come into the open.

"I should ask you the same question, why did you burst into our home like some kind or demented lunatic.I thought you wanted to kill me or something."

Jez had no idea as to his wife's demeanour but then realised she must have seen the car outside and flipped at seeing the carnage he had brought home. He reasoned it surely couldn't have anything to do with his other life, that was strictly private, of which he alone had access to.

Chapter 29

"Is it the car? I'm sorry I can explain." He couldn't but he wasn't thinking rationally but of course neither was his wife.

"what about the car"

Shit she hadn't seen it then what the hell was going on here, the question racing through his troubled mind.

"Are you seeing somebody else" her words were spoken so softly Jez asked her to repeat herself. She couldn't believe she had finally asked the question, but there it was. She repeated the words this time said with a little more authority and purpose.

"what sort of question is that for heavens sake"

"a question that I'd like you to answer and truthfully with none of your usual bullshit"

"no I'm not seeing anybody right now" he lied, his ego bruised "but if I was could you blame me"

"what's that supposed to mean?" she answered a little forthrightly but also realising where this avenue of enquiry was leading and in truth didn't want to go there but she had to see this out to the bitter end, of that much she was certain.

"look at yourself, you've become a mess, you've let yourself go, big time"

"so what your'e saying is I'm ugly, is that it" she coldly interjected "no I'm not saying that at all" again he didn't believe himself

"so what are you inferring, oh don't bother I already know I'm fat, is that it, I'm not sexy anymore" she stared into his eyes searching for some kind of reaction, positive or negative.

"you're fucking pathetic Jez, you know that, but I thought as we're bloody married we share everything, no secrets, for better or worse, as I recall and on that basis I don't deserve your shit"

"oh talking about shit what's that on the chair your sitting on" he suddenly felt relieved to have been able to change the subject and earn a brief respite, knowing she wouldn't let up, she was like a dog with a bloody bone, of that he knew, but how did she know about his extra marital activities, she was guessing he reassured himself. She had to be surely.

Mary suddenly felt chilled to the bone as she came to realise her seated position and dilemma over the chair. She hadn't masked the smell after all, she felt horrified at this latest twist of knowledge.

" I was ill this morning and had an accident ok? it happens, oh sorry I forgot you're so perfect you don't do those sort of things, only a fat bitch like me, can do such a horrid thing"

"you're beginning to sound hysterical, calm down"

"don't tell me to calm down and don't change the fucking subject, are you seeing someone?"

"look this is ridiculous, if you must know, I'm not" he was becoming used to lying but as he began to fidget in his chair Mary began also to wonder, if indeed there was an element of truth to her accusation.

"so what are you basing your argument on, have you seen me with someone or what"

"no I haven't"

"so there" his voice sounding a little too excited sensing triumph. He pushed onwards; feeling he was beginning to gain the upper hand, advantage to him.

"all this is in your imagination, just because you feel insecure doesn't give you the right to throw unfounded accusations my way. Your talking total bollocks Mary and you know it"

His words were sounding believable and in truth she knew she didn't have any real evidence to offer. Her thoughts raced back to her meeting with the Doctor and his words flooded through her mind like a tsunami.

Jez began to stand up realising his wife had been defeated, the expressionless look on her face telling him so. Little did he know her next retort would open up a huge can of worms the ramifications of which would be catastrophic and endless. It would change his life forever.

"what about the prostitutes?"

Chapter 30

Jez fell back into the settee, a look of total bewilderment forged across his now strained features. He knew instinctively that he had been well and truly sussed, found out, but how. If his wife knew of his dalliances with the ladies of the night, he could well and truly kiss his world, as he knew it, goodbye, adios, goodnight Vienna and as for her Father's inheritance, fat chance of ever seeing anything there come to fruition. He had to try to box clever, but his body language was already revealing his nefarious secrets. He knew it would be futile to remonstrate his innocence, he knew his wife had to have irrefutable proof, to the contrary, she wouldn't just come out and accuse him of such treachery, it wasn't her style, his head began to swim. He had to try. He had to.

" Look I don't know what to say, I don't know who you've been talking too, but this is complete and utter nonsense" A slight but nonetheless noticeable stammer to his voice and not altogether lost on his wife.

"if the look on your face and sound of your voice is anything to go by, I reckon it's a fair and accurate statement, a fair cop"

"so if this crap is true where's your proof, your evidence"

"you're not denying it then"

"yes I bloody well am,with bells on, oh don't tell me

you've been having a chin wag with Andrea, over a bottle of plonk, no doubt, you know she hates me and would love to split us up, she's always banging on to you about how you could do better. I wouldn't put it past her to stir up shit, its in her nature, she's nasty and you know it oh and I found your empty bottle upstairs along with the remains of your take away, tossed all over the bed, what? did you eat in your sleep or something; its bloody disgusting" A change of tact again, could he turn this around.

"if you came home more often than not, I wouldn't feel the need to eat and drink, like I do"

"so you're saying this is all my fault" a pained look on his face adding to his features.

Mary felt her throat constrict, how could he sit here and bareface lie to her, she knew without doubt by the mere way he protested, he was guilty on all accounts and pressed home her advantage.

"don't bring Andrea into this, it has nothing to do with her if you must know, but yes I have been told and reliably so. PROSTITUTES" she screamed the word directly into his face.

The effect was instantaneous, Jez looked a well and truly beaten man his head flinched as if hit by a train.

The pair sat in silence, waiting to see who would indeed make the next move, like a game of chess, but the stakes were much higher and they both knew it.

Jez broke the painful silence.

" so who is your star witness then" layered with not just a hint but a trowel of sarcasm.

" an elderly Doctor I met today at MacDonalds." She retorted with supercilious authority.

Jez suddenly burst into a fit of unreserved laughter,

"you're telling me you met a complete stranger and listened to a pile of horse shit about me. If I thought you were mad when you barged in, there's your proof. You've fucking lost it big time girl and you know it. Fucking Doctor, I've heard enough of this shit for one day. Fuck you Mary"

Jez began to rise from his seated position, fucking Doctor, the woman's gone completely mad, he concluded.

"how can you sit there......' he decided not to continue, in truth he couldn't be bothered his head ached and he decided a lay down on the bed upstairs complete with last nights take out appeared infinitely far more an attractive proposition than having to sit here and listen to this tortuous attack on his character. So what it may be true, but she had no proof, he reasoned. But as an after thought he added, "MacDonalds, enough said"

Mary felt for the first time a calmness enveloping her and a steely determination to finish this once and for all.

" I haven't finished yet, sit down" Her retort was fired with such ferocity Jez found himself promptly back in his seat again and staring back at a woman he barely recognized. Mary's face was flushed red with adrenaline and anger, her eyes were on fire, her fists clenched ready for another assault if required.

"I've sat here night after night alone when you've been out about acting like a single bloke, getting up to God knows what and you have the audacity to criticise me. Yes so what, I met someone today and you know what I totally believe him and no I have no proof but what he told me made complete sense" "so what else did this harbinger of doom tell you about me?"

"he told me you act the way you do, visiting prostitutes because you can't face up to your own inadequacies, your responsibilities which is the reason why you don't want children"

Mary not only looked elated she felt elated at this revelation. The look on her husbands face a complete picture, priceless. He sat motionless his mouth dropped open, Mary kinda knew how he felt. Her day had certainly been full of surprises, well there's one for you big boy she prided herself.

"and the worse thing about this is you have never once admitted it to me, your own bloody wife and I always wanted kids and all because you don't know how to be a Dad, talking of which you never ever mentioned your parents, your upbringing, you can't live in the past."

For what seemed an interminable age Jez sat with his mouth open, his body stiff all over, as if somehow he had lost sense and use of his faculties. He knew what Mary had just told him was inexplicably the truth. He could barely look after himself let alone a family, and he couldn't bring himself to talk about his own parents, he never knew his Dad and as for his Mum, she could go to hell, fucking alcoholic.But was that the reason he visited the prostitutes he wasn't so sure, maybe, he had never ever tried to rationalise his behaviour, question it, so long as nobody found out, nobody would be hurt, it was his problem and his alone. But not anymore. He knew instinctively the fight was over the truth was out, there seemed little use in denying it, Mary was that set that not even a hurricane would blow her off course. It was indeed time to face the music. At least damage limitation, Jez felt his Father in laws inheritance slipping through his fingers.

" I don't know what to say" he offered his hands upwards in an apologetic stance, it seemed futile. He thought Mary would burst into tears or something but she just sat in stony silence, beseeching him to continue.

" OK I admit i've been but just the once" Both he and Mary knew he was lying but as far as she was concerned once was once too often.

"you utter bastard, how could you" her voice a whisper as she struggled to keep the tears from flowing, she was damned if she was about to give him the satisfaction. Jez leant across to offer a comforting hand. " You have to understand how I feel"

"don't you fucking touch me, you make me sick, I hate you. Fuck off out off my house"

Her words stabbed at his heart. She continued as if he hadn't heard and needed telling over and over again.

"get out, get out" she began to scream the words at him." I want you out now" the emphasise on the word now.

Jez suddenly felt a rage of such intensity overwhelm him. He felt powerless to control it.

"Your house, your house" he screamed back " its my fucking house I pay the fucking bills not you, why don't you fuck off" and at the same time he reached for the empty wine bottle sitting unobtrusively on the coffee table. His hand circled the neck of the bottle his hands were sweating, not profusely but enough for him to grip the bottle even tighter than normally and with a look of complete madness about him he hurled the bottle with all his might.

The bottle flew through the air like a guided missile searching for its intended target and crashed wholly into the plasma television screen on the opposite wall. The noise on impact was deafening as the television screen shattered into a thousand pieces. Mary had worked her way into a standing position, in truth she wanted to leave, not the house but certainly this room.

Jez on seeing his beloved television's demise swung round to vent his now insatiable anger at his wife and with a curled fist slammed it into Mary's face, breaking her nose immediately. The force of the impact was so severe it also knocked her completely off balance and she crashed head first into the glass topped coffee table.

Jez stared down at Mary's seemingly lifeless body blood seeping from both her mouth and nose. A cold shudder enveloped him dowsing his anger and the realisation of what had just transpired becoming only too evident. Jez fell to his knees horrified at his actions. He tried to speak but no words formulated. A feeling of foreboding and guilt weighing heavily onto his sagging shoulders. He had just crossed the line and there was no going back. He reached out and felt her neck this time his hands sweating as though just retrieved from a shower or bath. Sweat fell heavily from his brow and stung his eyes. Her body felt warm and clammy to his touch and involuntarily he flinched. What did he expect, was she dead, he jumped up his revulsion making him want to vomit. He stared again at the prone body of his wife and for the very first time; his bravado escaping him, felt truly vulnerable and scared. He headed for the hallway and as he opened the front door he peered back and for a moment he thought he saw a leg move but couldn't be certain. The coward which he had always been but one which he had masked for so long rushed out of the house little knowing if he would ever set eyes on his wife again.

Chapter 31

Mary laid in a foetal position on the floor for how long she didn't know, she knew she had fallen unconscious after hitting her head on the coffee table. In truth she felt as if she'd been hit by a freight train. Except it hadn't been a train had it, it had been her husband. Her thoughts raced through her mind, what to do. She felt the taste of blood in her mouth, her face one side embedded in the plush carpet, the other already swollen, she couldn't feel her mouth, it felt as if she had been to the dentist and had all her wisdom teeth extracted at the same time and then some. But she knew again this was something else. Far worse than she could have ever imagined. Her husband had beaten her, in fact he could have killed her. Maybe I'm better off dead after all, she reasoned, she knew instinctively her life as she knew it was at its lowest ebb and she felt she was staring into the abyss. Her eyes were closed tight she was too scared to open them, what if her husband was standing over her, a demonic look on his face, a hammer in his hand too finish off his handy work. Somewhere in the recess of her mind she believed this wasn't so as she vaguely remembers hearing a car scream off the drive outside. It had to be her husband. She knew now how to hate someone. To hate without impunity. She wanted her husband too suffer ten fold her pain. Her suffering, her total humiliation. She was fat and very probably ugly, she certainly felt it, but she didn't deserve this, she felt the pain of every battered housewife in the land. In fact she wanted him dead, but to suffer, oh so dearly first. She wanted to cry, to cry for ever but her tears had run dry, she was beyond that point. She felt spent and exhausted, let me die please, I have nothing to live for, she pleaded inwardly. But the solace of the after life, if there was one, wouldn't come. No the grim reaper wouldn't be making an appearance today, no matter how much she yearned for it Life still goes on, but what life. She gingerly opened her eyes. At first she thought she had turned blind, she was enveloped by complete darkness, rising panic began to surge through her body, then colours began to converge her vision slowly coming back in to focus. Her breathing began to relax, her heart beat began to slow back down. As her vision gained full clarity once more, her eyes began to dance in a confused state. Searching but for what?. They came to rest upon what appeared at first glance to be a piece of strewn paper, realising its unimportance her eyes continued on, but something drew her eyes back to the discarded piece of paper. The paper lay inches from her outstretched hand and her aching head demanded her hand move in the direction of the paper. Her fingers encircled the paper and she felt something very familiar to the touch. She drew the paper, once encompassed in her grip and brought it up closer for a clearer view. She inhaled sharply, as recognition filtered to her brain, it was the Doctors calling card complete with the odd telephone number emblazoned upon it. The numbers seemed larger and bolder this time, perhaps that was her imagination, none the less she found herself staring with morbid fascination and little realising he had been the catalyst for her demise, thus far. Her eyes wandered again and this time set upon the portable telephone upended on the floor near her hand, in fact she couldn't remember seeing it previously, but she must still be slightly concussed, the thought didn't stop to trouble her. Before she had reason to doubt her actions, she had dialled the number on the card almost by memory alone, after all, she was no longer in control. The phone clicked into action, and was surreptitiously placed beside her ear. There was not even a ringing tone at the other end. "Ah Mary I've been expecting your call"

Chapter 32

"How did you know it was me?" but the words remained unspoken.

Mary tried to voice the words over and over as the Doctors words invaded her body. But her broken nose and swollen mouth contrived to prohibit her speech. Instead her ears amplified the sound, his words delving deeper and deeper.

"Mary I feel your pain and I know you are having difficulty in speaking right now. I am instructing you to just listen and do as I bid." The Doctor's words offered little comfort, why should they, but Mary felt compelled as he saw fit. To follow his instructions complicity and compliably.

" There is a car waiting for you outside, make your way to the front door where the driver will ably assist you"

The phone abruptly went dead. Not for a moment did Mary begin to question his motives or indeed where she was heading. She knew.

With another Herculean effort Mary found herself standing upright. The pain from her injuries momentarily subsided. Her head seemed no longer to ache. A huge dose of morphine would probably have had a similar effect. She was beyond caring, or of rational thought. She was at the front door in no time, her legs feeling light as a feather, she may as well have been walking on water. She caught a glimpse of her disfigured face in the hallway mirror and tossed the image to one side. It doesn't matter anymore. She knew where she was going.

As she exited her house she was warmly greeted by the same driver whom she had met earlier, this time he offered her a broad and caring smile, his offered hand she accepted with grace but in a dreamlike fashion. The door to the cab already open and in no time she had been warmly accepted once again into its inner sanctum. Mary fell immediately into a deep and comfortable sleep. With its occupant firmly ensconced the car pulled away effortlessly on its way at last to its true and final destination.

A cars horn blasted outside and immediately brought Mary round from her seemingly deep comatose state. She was seated at the same table she had sat earlier in the day at the MacDonalds restaurant and opposite her with his broad smile sat the Doctor.

"You may talk if you wish too, Mary, I do believe you have found your voice again"

"how did I get here, I can't remember, Jez and I argued, I know that much, but what am I doing here again"

Her voice was true and free of any encumbrance.

"you have asked for my help have you not" the Doctor replied calmly.

"I guess so, but I don't remember, how did I get here?", what am I doing here?"

"as I have informed you, you asked for my help my intervention and I am offering it to you, all you need to do is ask for it to my face directly."

Mary's day had for all intents and purposes been a roller coaster ride of unfurling events, she no longer wanted to question anything. She felt she had lost her sanity, was she dreaming, it all felt so surreal.

"do I have your answer?" the Doctor probed.

Mary answered unwittingly it felt. She must be dreaming, this day, none of it had happened. I'll wake and all this has been a nightmare. None of this is real anyway. She felt she was standing on the edge of a cliff ready to leap off. One foot then the next, then!!

"yes I want your help"

"say please" the doctor tormenting her just a little.

" please I want your help"

" then you may have it my dear"

He withdrew his hand to his side and then brought his clenched fist back to the table. He opened up his hand and offered to Mary what appeared to be a small pill. A paracetamol perhaps. His other hand came into view guiding a cup with what appeared to be full with water.

"Drink this as a sign of your acceptance and willingness" he offered.

"what is it?" Mary questioned.

"a little sedative to help you sleep tonight, after all youv'e had quite an extraordinary day. Please if you will"

He pushed the pill and drink further forward.

Mary hesitated, her foot dangling over the precipice

"it will only help I promise, please" the doctor pressed encouragement.

Chapter 33

With suddenly shaking hands Mary brought the pill to her lips and voluntarily sniffed at it. The pill offered her nose no scent but then Mary suddenly realised her nose had been broken and having never been in this predicament before couldn't make up her mind as to the authenticity of the pill. Her hands still trembling she placed the pill into her mouth and rested it onto her protruding tongue. It was tasteless.

The Doctor pushed forward once again the cup of water.

"if you will Mary, you have absolutely nothing to fear" This time his voice seemed to have a calming influence over her and she noticed immediately her hand steadied. The pill languishing on her tongue suddenly gave up a peppermint odour, which caressed the insides of her mouth, salivating she took hold of the cup and drew it upwards towards her mouth. She eyed the Doctor opposite for any sign of skulduggery but in return he offered a benevolent and continuous smile suggesting all was right in the world. She took a large gulp from the cup and swallowed the pill at the same time closing her eyes fearing hell or an otherwise ungodly catastrophe was about to descend upon her.

Nothing happened.

She cautiously opened her eyes wondering what

might befall her. Instead the Doctor simply smiled back at her. Nothing seemingly had changed.

" there that wasn't so difficult was it, after all. What did you expect, fire and brimstone to rain down on you from above. My head suddenly to grow hideous horns. Hell and damnation to befall upon you." The Doctor stifled a laugh and dipped his shoulders." I dare say you've been reading too many horror stories or I dare say further, watching too much television. These horror stories really will keep you up all night. This isn't Hollywood Mary just a poor soul crying out for help and you have just given yourself a huge slice of it"

"I don't understand, I don't feel any different" Mary placed the cup down onto the table.

"what indeed were you expecting Mary. It is after all just a pill it will help you sleep very well tonight. To answer your question truthfully Mary you know not how you feel at this present time, doubtless you're mind is somewhat confused, of course the beating administered by your husband was appalling and in due time he shall be visited and accept his punishment of that you can be certain, but for know I shall wish you a fond farewell"

" how did you know about my husband hitting me"

'questions, questions, always questions, my dear, your face alone tells its own story, who else could have given you such a beating. You said yourself you had argued tonight. If you do not believe me, then take a look in the mirror behind me, or if you prefer when you are safe and sound in your own home."

"but"

"no more I refuse to answer, suffice it to say you are in good hands and I shall take care of you, all you need to do is go home, open up a bottle of wine or two, if the fancy takes you, and see what the morning brings you, however you must let your husband back into your marital bed when he returns." The Doctor stood over Mary

" I have, again, seen to it the cab will take you home, everything has for now been taken care of. Please be on your way" He addressed Mary with a somewhat conciliatory tone, he was bringing this meeting to an abrupt close and his dismissive behaviour left Mary with a bewildering feeling and too many questions unanswered, how did he know about Jez and as for his whereabouts that was anybody's guess, and too let him into her bed, fat chance of that matey. But one thing was for sure she suddenly wanted to be rid of this Doctor or whoever he was, she definitely didn't want to see him again. Perhaps it was best to leave.

She felt silly and stupid, asking a stranger for help and for what, her life was in ruins she was beyond help now. She concluded the dear old good Doctor was nothing short of a looney tune, he probably hailed from some nut house somewhere and had taken a leave of absence, either way he was probably just a bit lonely, well enough was enough she had given enough of her time to this little charade it was indeed time to go home. As she began to remember the beating administered by her husband, she decided she didn't care if she ever set eyes on him again.

Chapter 34

Mary woke as the car door was pulled open. Smiling back at her and proffering his hand the same cab driver she had been chauffeured by the previous two occasions. Mary shook her head in disbelief, she couldn't remember leaving the restaurant let alone getting back into this cab, all she wanted to do was to be rid of the Doctor once and for all. She wished she'd never met him, but then the same could be said of her errant husband. God what a day it had turned out to be. Certainly not one for the record books, best left alone and consigned to history. Still she was safe, at home, at least for the time being anyway. Once inside Mary found herself staring at the inside of the fridge and low and behold sat two bottles of white wine. She couldn't recall seeing them there the previous evening, perhaps Jez had brought them home. Her mind swiftly recalled the Doctor's words about being home and drinking a bottle or two of wine, she shook her head vehemently, the Doctor had gone she wouldn't be seeing him again either, that was for sure, but as for these two bottles of wine, after the day i've had, they'll do just nicely, she purred to herself, and armed with a clean glass and bottle opener set about her task to consume the bottles contents with vigour and relish.

Her last thought as she fell into her bed was that she hadn't locked the front door, she didn't want her husband to come home she had intended in locking him out, not just tonight but for good, but as she pulled the duvet over her head, the alcohol from the two bottles letting her brain know that come the morning she would again inherit the mother of all hangovers, she let a deep sleep overtake her thought of going downstairs and locking the door, as she slurringly whispered, 'fuck you Jez I can't be bothered.'

Chapter 35

The suns rays began to filter through the bedrooms curtains denoting that morning was well and truly under way. The occupant of the double bed blinked furiously at this untimely intervention, it can't be time to get up, he thought angrily. His head began to bang furiously as if a thousand marching bands had somehow invaded his brain and he sat up a little too quickly a feeling of wanting to be sick came to the fore. He quickly flung his legs out of the bed and stood up. He definitely wanted to throw up big time. Where was he, he didn't know but the burning issue at hand was to find a toilet and be darned quick about it. As if on auto pilot he made his way into an ensuite toilet and promptly fell to his knees his head precariously hanging over the toilet bowl.

As Jez began to yield last night's food and alcohol consumption, he let his mind wander over the previous evenings events. They were vague at best, but he certainly remembered hitting his wife and through his guilt and anguish had driven off in a blind fit of panic and literally dived into the first pub he found across town and descended into a marathon event of drinking, in truth he wanted to drink himself into oblivion. And he had. The rest of the evening was a complete mystery, a total blank. His guilt began to resurface as his thoughts came back to Mary. For all her faults, she didn't deserve that. He stepped back into the bedroom and noticed for the first time another body in the bed. Where was he, what had he done. Who was she. The thoughts racing through his mind, god some bloody bimbo, I guess. I better find my clothes and get the hell out of here whilst the goings still good, he decided.

The body stirred and Jez stood rigid and firmly still. He didn't want to wake her up, its was best if he just left. The duvet fell onto the floor as the woman tossed her arm out, had he woken her. The light filtering through the curtains gave Jez just enough natural light to view the room and in particular the double bed. A young girl lay totally naked, upon the bed. Her face a picture of breathtaking beauty. Her eyes were shut tight, she was still asleep. Jez stepped cautiously over to the bed to take a better look. He gasped inwardly as his eyes fixed upon the girls total nakedness. God she looked serenely beautiful, another thought crossed his mind, God I must have fucked this girl and I can't remember a dammed thing about it. As he stared intently at her nakedness his eyes noticing the girls firm and rounded breasts, her legs slightly parted and he couldn't help himself taking a look down below. Her womanhood was completely bald, he wanted to bury his face into her very own private place and as he thought this he began to become extremely aroused, she can't have been any older than 18 years of age. Another thought suddenly struck him what if she was younger, god I'm in enough trouble as it is, this is the last thing I bloody need. Her Mum and Dad are probably next door. But his ardour kept him rooted to the spot. His erection he know held as hard as he had ever been in his life and he suddenly noticed she had what appeared to be golden blond hair.

It was no good he had to take a better look and dammed the consequences. He stepped back from the bed and pulled back the curtains. His jaw fell to the floor 'oh god'

Chapter 36

It couldn't be, his eyes were immediately drawn to what looked a blemish on her otherwise immaculate face. He stepped quickly back to the bed to investigate further his heart beginning to race. He peered intently at this vision of complete beauty and his eyes came to rest on a mole of some description on the girls face. His heart rate pounding, he leant down so close that he could smell the girls beautiful aroma, he could almost hear her heart beat, he could hear his own, that was for sure, it pounded in his ears, alarm bells ringing.

'It can't be' he whispered. He was staring at a mole on her skin, nothing unusual in that, but the mole a slightly different shade of colour from the rest of her body, was formed in the shape of a heart. The same as his wife's.

'it can't be'

He repeated his words again and jumped back from the bed. 'No way I must be dreaming' He threw his eyes quickly around the room and realised he had been here before. He ran to the bathroom and his fears were recognised, he was without mistake, at home in his own bedroom.

He stood in his en suite fear coursing through his body. He suddenly screamed as he heard a voice whisper his name from the bedroom

'JEZ'

The voice was not of an angel, it belonged to Mary his wife.

He threw himself back into the bedroom, fully expecting to see his wife of old languishing in her pit. Fully realising that what had just transpired was a dream or through his alcoholic state had imagined it. He stood in the bedroom and his knees nearly gave way at the sight beholding upon him. The body he thought he had dreamed was real and alive as he was.

"Mary is that you" his words sounding strained and uncomfortable.

"what do you think", her reply sounded silky and sexy. He couldn't answer, this was mad, so unreal, unbelievable. The girl addressing him instinctively knew, to the contrary as she woke up. She ran her hands along her body caressing every inch of her body, her eyes remained steadfastly closed, heightening her own arousal. She didn't want to look just yet, her pleasure anticipating by her touch alone. She parted her legs ever so slowly, raised her knees and began to caress her inner sanctum, her fingers relishing her inner warmth and moistness. She lifted a finger to her mouth and smiled her teeth were startlingly white and immaculately straight. She knew yes of course she knew it all fell into place. The Doctor.

"Yes it is me Jez come over to me and let me touch you" she invited.

In a dreamlike state Jez came and stood beside his wife. She let out her hand and took his manhood into her silky hand and began to caress him ever so slowly and expertly.

"yes its me"

Jez stood and watched as his wife caressed him slowly backwards and forwards.

"I don't get this" was all he could stammer

Smiling serenely she offered "don't think about it lets just say we are going to start our lives again"

She stopped what she was doing and Jez let out an abrupt sigh.

"but, from now on, of course it shall be on my terms" she warned him "from now on you will do exactly what I say" and playfully pat him on his backside. "Before I ravage you're huge friend here, can you bring in the full length mirror from the bathroom, your'e old mirror, I want to view myself in my mirror"

Dumbfounded and confused and like a nodding dog Jez acquiesced and ran to the bathroom to retrieve the full length portable mirror that he himself always stood in front of admiring his own physique. It was Mary's now. He didn't care.

Mary stood by the side of the bed her body firm, her breasts protruding without a sag in sight, her legs long and shapely, her long blond hair caressing her backside. Her eyes shut in anticipation and smiling she demanded Jez put the mirror in front of her body.

"come on quickly, I can't wait any longer" she demanded

Jez stood the mirror where he was instructed his manhood so rigid now, that the pain of it made him think at any minute now he might faint.

Something caught his eye and he bent down to retrieve it. It was some kind of business card and as he viewed it, the numbers began to form into letters right in front of his own eyes. The card read DR LEVI.

His voice began to tremble as he voiced uncertainty the words to his wife

" ok you can open your eyes now"

Chapter 37

Outside a black car sat on the driveway its engine idling quietly. The driver sat expressionless in the front. Aware of his clients demands to be stoically quiet at this moment in time. After all, the driver smiled inwardly he had been here a million times before, his client liked to say goodbye personally to his brethren.

The elderly gentlemen sat in the back of the car and peered up to the bedrooms window a knowing smile etched across his handsome features.

"Business here has been concluded it is time to move on"

"Did the lady accept the pill your highness?" the driver enquired a little nervously.

"you know full well not to interrupt me but I shall this once answer you, but of course"

and added "totally pointless, mind you, but I do like to have fun" and he began to laugh. A sinister sound emanating throughout the car's interior.

"I don't understand" the driver interjected.

" My dear fellow, you never do. Let me explain to you for the millionth time. The pill I offer is purely a symbol, an act of one's acceptance to my power, I like to see peoples reactions when absolutely nothing happens. It is all part of the fun. However my dear Mary did seem a trifle concerned on accepting her pill.

The look on her face was quite remarkable. Perhaps I should have revealed to her my true identity at that point, now that would have been fun and a first."

The Doctor waved his hand to dismiss the driver from this seemingly banal banter. It was time to venture onwards.

"what about her husband, what do you have planned for him?" the driver asked quizzically, mindful of how far he dare push.

"all in good time, all in good time" came an irritated reply. The doctor retrieved from his waistcoat pocket one of many blank business cards and as he viewed the card, his manicured hands slowly began to change shape. Each finger began to elongate, his nails becoming razor like talons. The business card was blank, but soon lettering appeared with the name DR LEVI firmly visible and as his eyes turned from blue to a crimson deep fiery red the name changed to DEVIL. At the exact time Jez laid his eyes on the business card found on the floor in his bedroom.

The Doctor moved a gnarled talon to his head and felt complete as he lovingly stroked the twin horns above his deathly head.

He reached across the seat and held in his claw a bejewelled trinket box and a forked tongue caressed his cracked lips in anticipation as his talons lovingly caressed the boxes exterior.

Chapter 38

As Mary opened her eyes, simultaneously the beautiful couple fell to their knees. Their screams dancing a pirouette becoming louder and louder. Mary threw her hands to her face and as her fingers delved she vomited all over the stricken body of her now dead husband, the victim of a sudden and overwhelming heart attack..

The Devil, outside, opened up the trinket box and there before him, on offer, the boxes red satin interior exposed to the voyeur, contained a pair of the most beautiful hazel eyes his darkened pits had ever set their miserable, sinister sights on. He roared a sound from his disfigured orifice, his blackened teeth beset with sharp fangs, a sound he knew well would be heard in the depths of hell and took pleasure knowing their screams would last an eternity. The car's exhaust blew fire from its pipe and with the wheels tearing at the tarmac drive, screamed up the road, fire beginning to lick at the windows, from within, its course known only to the inhabitant, the next Town or City ready to yield its immeasurable number of wishful victims to continue satiating his lust and desire for more deserving souls.

The I Wish You Well Chronicles continues with the next breathtaking and nerve jangling installment ''silver lining'' but for those of you with a nervous disposition, beware, take note and especially be careful ''what you wish for''

Sometime in the distant past.

Chapter 1

The young woman sits staring intently at her diamond ring. A gift she gratefully and thankfully received earlier in the day. It was just so typical of her boyfriend, oops she corrects herself, fiancee, she can scarcely believe it, but her eyes are definitely not lying to her Ryan Taylor her intended had turned up at her work place carrying an over the top gargantuan bouquet of flowers, in fact she had no idea where she would put them in her one bed roomed apartment, they were that big and she had no room, but of course she would find room. But there he stood in a powerful looking charcoal grey suit scrubbed to the nines his hair immaculately barbered, she scarcely recognized him in all his refinery especially as the last time she had seen him, 24 hours ago, his hair languished around his shoulders in a neat pony tail. Ryan was trying for a scholarship in acting and never had any money, or so it seemed, and she always had her hand in her pocket on account her employers paid fairly handsomely. Elena Tomlinson worked on the floor of Sacks on 5th Avenue for a leading cosmetics firm and Elena knew she was going places.

So there he stood, the memory still fresh as she fingers with her ring. It fitted just perfectly, how had he known her finger size, a question she would ask him tomorrow.

In full view of everyone who just happened to be in the immediate vicinity of where she stood, he fell to his knees immediately in front of her, he placed the overburdening flowers at her feet, and from his suit pocket he retrieved a small red box with a ribbon neatly tied on top. With smiling eyes he hands the box over to her and waits like an obedient puppy dog for his answer to a question he has of yet not asked. Elena accepts the box, deep down realizing what the box contains. He asks her to open it as she holds and stares at it for an interminable age. A disquiet descends upon the shops floor as all eyes it feels are locked in to Elena's orbit. She is acutely aware of the silence surrounding her and she feels her skin beginning to redden, with nervous embarrassment but excitement none the less.

Without thought it seems she opens the box with trembling fingers the ribbon falling to the floor. The ribbon falls and as it lands is quickly and expertly removed by a coworker, standards to be fair must be kept up and littering the floor just wont do, no matter what the occasion. Elena hasn't noticed, she is too preoccupied with the cluster diamond ring on show.

She hears the words as if somewhere in the far away distance. 'Will you marry me? Elena'

She looks down upon Ryan's handsome features his blue eyes shining like beacons. Her hands still trembling she reaches down to find his warm and comforting hand.

"Yes I will" almost a whisper emanates from her mouth. A smile beginning to form as the enormity of the situation begins to dawn. The realisation she wants to spend the rest of her life with this young, athletic and talented young man .

A voice from behind her barks aloud for the now bewitched audience of shoppers and workers alike, to hear 'She says yes'

The floor erupts with a cacophony of whoops and cheers. People hugging each other and clapping one and others backs.

Elena burst into tears.

She pulls herself away from her reverie. The remainder of the day had flown by. Unfortunately Ryan had to attend an audition the same evening otherwise he would have spent the evening no doubt with her. Instead she had been treated to a meal by her employers and 8 staff members had been royally treated to a lavish feast with drinks thrown in at Lucio's, Elena's favourite Italian restaurant in the heart of Little Italy. Courtesy of Chanel.

Elena now sat fidgeting in her seat as the train came to a stop. She looked up and realized she was on her complete own. She looked at her watch and gasped at the time 10:30pm My God she exclaimed inwardly where has the day gone.

Chapter 2

The trains doors open revealing to the oncoming passengers an almost empty carriage all except the young lady fidgeting and giggling to herself. The man and only passenger enters the trains enclosure and as he passes the lady he detects a faint smell of alcohol infused with a wisp of expensive perfume. Perfect. He takes the seat directly opposite the lady and stares intently at her.

Elena looks up as the doors open and notices the scruffy individual as he enters the carriage. To her utter and total annoyance he sits opposite her. She wants to look away to avoid this intrusion. She is suddenly aware of how lonely and vulnerable she has become in a nano second of time. Ryan's voice in the back of her mind always reminding her never to travel the train on her own at night time, it's a dangerous place.

Her eyes can't help but notice the tramp like look of the man who judging by his sodden appearance would be in his late 40's. His denim jeans are black with worn in dirt and grease and oil. Tears and rips up and down the legs revealing parts of flesh which haven't seen a bar of soap let alone water in weeks. The rain mack grey dirty and yellowing with age especially around the cuffs.

She finally meets his eyes and fear begins to coarse through her body. She bites hard on her lips to stifle the scream welling up inside.

His eyes are black and glazed and seemingly lifeless but seem to bore into her own eyes with such intensity, as if searching for her soul. His head rocks back and forward rhythmically encouraging her to dance with him. His hair is long dark unwashed and falls to his lap. His unkempt beard of similar description and length. The smell emanating from his body a mixture of not having washed for months and urine causing Elena to nearly retch.

She pulls her eyes away and searches the carriage for evidence of other souls, but realises she is on her own.

The trains rumblings along the tracks increases as the train gains momentum. The carriage sways in time to the trains powerful forward motion.

Elena slowly stands up avoiding again any eye contact with the man and purposefully moves to the far end of the carriage. The train rumbles on it lights flickering as surges of electricity run through it.

Elena looks to the floor and silently begins to pray for the next stop to arrive. She knows its not her stop but she has to get off no matter what, to breath in fresh air. She is beginning to feel claustrophobic. She hears a rustling, an alien noise, her heart beginning to beat a little faster. She looks up and the man is sitting opposite her once again, his eyes again searching.

The man sniffs the air, he can feel the woman's nervousness, he lifts the collar of his mack, he feels himself becoming aroused. He licks his lips slowly he wants her to see him. He begins to salivate. His drug filled brain completely mashed.

The train comes to a stop and its doors thunders open. The lady has already vacated her seat and out onto the platform in a flash. He places his hand into his coat pocket and feels the metal object and caresses it lovingly............ Time to play.

Elena steps onto the platform and begins to panic again, the exit stairs are at the end. Of course she realises she exited at the wrong stop, but she just had to get off. She steps off towards the stairs with a briskness to her walk, refusing to look back into the carriage to see if the man is still seated in his chair. There is still nobody about. The train exits the station and into the dark tunnel, continuing its own journey. Elena is unaware.

She reaches the bottom of the platforms stairs and as she places her foot on the bottom step, she jumps as a heavy hand grabs her hard on her shoulder and swings her around. The man with the dark eyes a satanic look about him stares aggressively back his mouth open revealing yellow and stained teeth the two front teeth jagged and uneven. A noise resembling a laugh but to Elena more of a pitiful howl escapes his mangy dirty orifice. A look that told her exactly where her day was going.

Chapter 3

An hour or so later the precinct sergeant receives a call from a distressed holiday maker and within minutes a team is dispatched to the vicinity where the call came from.

Mike Espinosa stares horridly down at the dead victim on the floor. A young lady in her early twenties. He already knows her body has been violated, brutally raped the blood coagulating around her neck from the razor sharp instrument that has gutted her throat. Her eyes staring back. Dead.

He knows there will be no id found on the body, another John Doe for the Cities Morgue. A sparkle and his eyes fixate on the cluster diamond ring sitting prettily on the dead girls wedding finger. Shit.

He calls it in. The young copper is distraught with grief as the sergeant answers his call. He recently moved here from Chicago. It's the third killing in as many weeks. Fuck what is this place. He controls his rising anger.His training keeping his voice calm and clear.

'Yeah serge, another to add to the collection. It's definitely him again. Same MO the works and recent too, the body is still warm, right under our noses.'

'Are you sure its him, come on, where this bloody city is concerned, murders are becoming two a dime' the serge replies.

'yep I'm near the subway on Penn and 34th Street and Eighth' 'The subway killer again, no doubt about it'

'ah well' the sergeant replies 'wait for the squad boys to show up and come back and file your report tonight. Welcome to the Big Apple Mike, good old NewYork City in the year of our Lord 1979'

The line went dead.

Printed in Great Britain
by Amazon